Holmes and Watson:

An American Adventure

~

David Ruffle

First edition published in 2015
© Copyright 2015
David Ruffle

The right of David Ruffle to be identified as the authors of this work has been asserted by him in accordance with the Copyright, Designs and Patents Act 1998.

All rights reserved. No reproduction, copy or transmission of this publication may be made without express prior written permission. No paragraph of this publication may be reproduced, copied or transmitted except with express prior written permission or in accordance with the provisions of the Copyright Act 1956 (as amended). Any person who commits any unauthorised act in relation to this publication may be liable to criminal prosecution and civil claims for damage.

All characters appearing in this work are fictitious. Any resemblance to real persons, living or dead, is purely coincidental. The opinions expressed herein are those of the authors and not of MX Publishing.

Paperback ISBN 978-1-78092-782-4
ePub ISBN 978-1-78092-783-1
PDF ISBN 978-1-78092-784-8

Published in the UK by MX Publishing
335 Princess Park Manor, Royal Drive, London, N11 3GX
www.mxpublishing.com

Cover layout and construction by
www.staunch.com

Also by David Ruffle

Sherlock Holmes and the Lyme Regis Horror
Sherlock Holmes and the Lyme Regis Horror (expanded 2nd Edition)
Sherlock Holmes and the Lyme Regis Legacy
Holmes and Watson: End Peace
Sherlock Holmes and the Lyme Regis Trials
The Abyss (A Journey with Jack the Ripper)
A Twist of Lyme
Sherlock Holmes: The Lyme Regis Trilogy (Illustrated Omnibus Edition)
Another Twist of Lyme
A Further Twist of Lyme
Sherlock Holmes and the Scarborough Affair (with Gill Stammers)

For Children

Sherlock Holmes and the Missing Snowman (illustrated by Rikey Austin)

As editor and contributor

Tales from the Stranger's Room (Vol.1)
Tales from the Stranger's Room (Vol. 2)

For Gill

Hyde Park 1890's

Chapter One

The year 1897 had been a relatively quiet one for my friend, Mr Sherlock Holmes. Although he was still in demand from all quarters by those who wished to make use of his especial skills, he could at this juncture of his life afford to select with care the cases he wished to look in to. One of the cases he investigated during the course of that year was an adventure I have chronicled elsewhere as 'The Devil's Foot', but in that particular instance the mountain came to Mahomet as the seemingly bizarre events that occurred took place within the vicinity of the cottage we had hired for the duration of a Cornish holiday that Holmes desperately needed. His health had caused me endless worry and a lengthy consultation with the renowned Dr Moore Agar of Harley Street confirmed my own diagnosis that Sherlock Holmes would benefit enormously from an extended holiday where murder and crime would not see fit to rear their heads.

He had told me once that work was the best antidote to everything and anything that ailed humankind and once more he was proved to be right and possibly, more astute, with regard to his own well-being than any Harley Street doctor. Refreshed, back in our Baker Street rooms, he waited for those crimes to come along that promised to be more than commonplace both in their commission and in their subsequent solution.

One spring morning I found Holmes seated at the breakfast table in a surprisingly ebullient mood. Often morose and quiet at breakfast, assuming he actually deigned to partake in the meal, this particular morning he was positively garrulous.

"Ah, Watson, you have risen at last. It is a glorious morning. What say we take a stroll to Hyde Park?"

"Good morning, Holmes. You seem especially cheery today; perhaps you have a case newly come to hand?"

"No, no case."

"A cryptograph then? Sent through the post in the hope you can solve its intricacies? I believe your exuberance must be related to the opened post lying on the basket-chair."

"Well deduced, my boy. This missive in particular," he answered with a flourish, holding both the letter and envelope above his head in a dramatic fashion. "It will, I believe have the effect of lifting me out of the doldrums of my enforced inactivity."

"As long as it doesn't require you to overexert yourself Holmes, your constitution is still in a weakened state."

"Nonsense, my boy. I am as strong as an ox, no doubt due to your ministrations."

"Which you usually ignore, Holmes!"

"Be that as it may, gulp down your coffee, Watson and let's take a turn in the park."

I protested that I had hardly touched the ham and eggs that Mrs Hudson had provided much less made a start on the coffee, but as often with Holmes, my protestations were in vain and in a few minutes I found myself donning an overcoat and bowler and following a retreating Holmes down Baker Street.

The spectacle, taken as just a spectacle, of London society airing itself in surely the pleasantest of London's parks is quite a sight indeed. There were were many, many carriages, landaus, barouches, victorias, curricles and private hansoms and horses of grand bearing competing against each other to entice the most favourable comments from the bystanders and strollers who flooded the park. There was not a shabby-looking turn-out to be seen. It is one of the worst of social misdemeanours to send a carriage and pair into the Park indifferently accoutred.

While we walked I endeavoured to draw out from my companion a little more about the contents of the letter which had so lifted his spirits, but to no avail.

"It can wait a while, Watson. Let us concentrate for the time being on the benefits this exercise will bring us, wonderful day for such a stroll is it not?"

"I cannot argue the point, Holmes."

It was to be some four hours before we returned to our rooms. Although I had not contemplated such exercise as part of the day I had planned for myself I would have been the first to admit it had left me spiritually and physically refreshed, certainly more so than the projected game of billiards with Thurston at the club. I settled down with the newspaper that had been delivered in our absence and noticed Holmes reading through his letter once more. I threw the paper down and looked up at him.

"Would you care to enlighten me now, Holmes?"

"I can see I will have no peace until I do so," he said, with a smile. "The letter is from Wilson Hargreave of the New York Police Bureau, you have heard me mention him before no doubt?"

"I cannot say I have ever heard you mention the name, Holmes."

"Perhaps not. I first made his acquaintance when I offered the NYPB my assistance during the so-called 'Jack the Ripper' murder of April 1891. The case was reported in the newspapers here, you may recall the details?"

"I have a vague remembrance. But this was just before your final confrontation with Moriarty surely?"

"Indeed it was. All I could do to assist initially was to apprise him of my suspicions regarding the murder. After my flight from Moriarty's henchmen I was able to pitch up in New York and offer my aid in person."

"You were in America? This is news to me. You have kept so much from me and I have to say I have never been able to puzzle out why."

"It has always been in my mind to fully apprise you of all my activities during that time and rest assured my friend I will do so in the fullness of time. By the time I arrived in New York a man had already been arrested, charged and tried for the crime."

"The right man?"

"In my view and many others, very far from the right man. Ameer Ben Ali was the unfortunate man and as far as I could ascertain, the evidence linking him to the crime was virtually non-existent and the so-called evidence which did exist was circumstantial in the extreme. Thanks to testimony from doctors who made claims that could not be supported by medical tests at the time, Ben Ali was tried and convicted of second degree murder and sentenced to life imprisonment, despite his well-founded claims of innocence. However, a group of reformers pointed out instances of police misconduct in the investigation and evidence to support Ben Ali's innocence. The group was able to prove the NYPB had made no attempt to find the missing key to the locked room or the unidentified man who witnesses claimed the victim had last been seen with the night before."

"A shocking miscarriage of justice, Holmes. Where does the missing key come into it? Remember, I only have a vague memory of this event."

"The victim, Carrie Brown was found in a room of the East River Hotel, in reality no more than a squalid lodging house. She was a prostitute of some years and this fact coupled with the mutilation of the body sent the press into a frenzy declaring that 'Jack the Ripper' was now at work in their city. Nonsense of course, but that has never stopped the press before."

"I am puzzled as to why this Ameer Ben Ali was convicted on such flimsy evidence."

"The city fathers demanded a quick solution. Hargreave's superior, Captain Byrnes was just the man to supply them with one."

"Are you saying that this unfortunate man was framed?"

"I would not go as far as to say that, but Byrnes undoubtedly reacted under the pressure forced upon him and once Ben Ali was arrested, the investigation was considered closed."

"And the unfortunate Ben Ali, what of him?"

"He still languishes in the state penitentiary."

"I deduce therefore that this letter from Wilson Hargreave details some new evidence that has come to light that possibly justifies whatever theory you may have expounded six years ago."

"Your deductions are wrong my dear fellow, it is an invitation to train his up and coming detectives in their art. A chance for me to pass on whatever knowledge and skills I possess to students who are hopefully only too willing to learn my ways and methods."

"How? A correspondence course?"

"No, Watson, I shall be required to be in New York in person."

"Hence your uncharacteristic cheeriness. When do you take up your post?"

"As soon as I am physically able."

"When do you expect to be back, I assume you will return to these shores at some point?"

"We will be back in six months if all proceeds smoothly."

"We?"

"Indeed, I am lost without my Boswell."

"I may have plans of my own, Holmes which do not include sea voyages and the delights or otherwise of the city of New York."

"Come now, Watson, what plans? You scarcely stir yourself at all these days unless it should be for days of interminable cricket watching or I am sure, equally interminable games of billiards with Thurston and his cronies. Fresh sea air, foreign climes…a grand adventure."

I had never been fond of sea voyages, always finding them rather dull affairs. My last experience of such voyaging had been aboard the troop ship *Orontes*, my health at that time had almost irretrievably broken down and the time spent on board was tempered by my illness and the feeling that I had left my best years behind me on the plains of Afghanistan. Although Holmes's words had some resonance for me, I wondered how I would be able to make use of my time in New York whilst Holmes played schoolmaster. I was sure that I would not be held up as an example of deductive skills to these police students. However, I had always found that refusing any of Holmes's requests was exceedingly difficult so, as often before, I acquiesced.

"I hope I don't regret it, but I will throw in my lot with you."

"Good man. How long do you need to put any affairs in order?"

"Sadly, not very long at all."

"Excellent. I will contact the steamship company and establish a time to travel and then wire Hargreave accordingly. New York will astound you, Watson as will our American cousins."

"If I am to be domiciled there for six months," I grumbled light-heartedly, "then I truly hope so."

SS Bremen

Chapter Two

I had no firm idea of what I needed to pack; six months is a long time to be away and Holmes's notion that we buy completely new outfits when we arrived in America did not sit comfortably with me, although, I could see the logic of it. I had become accustomed over the previous weeks to the appealing thought of being domiciled in America, but I really could not entertain the notion of becoming American through my attire. This did not appear to be a problem for Holmes, for whom packing was perfunctory and simple; he proposed to take very little other than a change of clothes sufficient for the journey of a few days.

Financially, I was what could be termed comfortably off due to wise investment, the occasional welcome wins at the racetracks of England and the monies that my chronicling of Holmes's adventures brought in, but I was still a little worried how far my finances would stretch in New York and its environs, particularly if I were to purchase whole new outfits! No matter how many times Holmes attempted to reassure me in this regard I still had misgivings which I hoped would be laid to rest eventually.

Holmes had secured our passage on the *SS Bremen* which would set sail from the port of the same name on June 5th and was due to reach New York on the 17th. We were to meet the ship on its stopover at Southampton. This was in fact the ship's maiden voyage which I sincerely hoped would not be indicative of teething problems. We had received welcome news from Wilson Hargreave prior to our departure, namely that monies had been made available to Holmes at Cox & Co, his bank, to enable him to purchase a first-class ticket for the vessel of his choice. This generous gesture was also extended to a companion, if Holmes decided to bring a guest for the duration. The letter also stated that all lodgings and board would be paid for by the NYPB, this again was extended to include a guest of Holmes.

"A very generous gesture indeed," I opined.

"I believe they also offer a plentiful salary for my perceived teaching skills. Sorry, Watson, but that does not extend to you, my friend," he laughed.

"Perhaps I will find temporary work teaching writing skills," I retorted.

"*Touché*, Watson."

On the morning of June 7th we said our goodbyes to Mrs Hudson, who did not betray whether our going was a sad occasion or one that she had perhaps been looking forward to! She had intimated to me that she was determined to fully spring clean our rooms as it was something that had been denied to her in the past. Holmes however had got wind of this plan and had stated in no uncertain terms that he wanted nothing touched, rearranged or otherwise tampered with. Graciously, he granted permission for a little light dusting which Mrs Hudson acknowledged with a grimace that she reserved for special occasions.

Our trunks had been sent on ahead to the port of Southampton which certainly made our journey to that fair town a lot easier. I was unsure of the size of *SS Bremen*, imagining something on the scale of the *Orontes*, but I let out an involuntary gasp when I laid my eyes on her. She was beautiful and certainly more streamlined than I would have thought possible. The funnels glinted in the midday sun with a striking display of splendour and the ship seemed to fill the whole of my vision. I estimated her length at five-hundred feet although I was to find out from the information sheet in the cabin it was slightly longer. The gangway swayed alarmingly as the passengers boarded and I gripped the handrail as firmly as I could.

We both declared our cabins to be most satisfactory indeed; the NYPB budget was abundant enough to provide us with accommodation in the first-class section. The next few days would certainly find us in the lap of luxury. With whistles and shouts galore the *SS Bremen* steamed out of the port. The study of human nature as exhibited on an ocean steamer is naturally one of the first things to engage one's attention, after the crowds on the pier are no longer distinguishable and the shores of our native land are swiftly receding from view. With a little stretch of imagination, aided by incidents of family history unwittingly overheard and the mirror in which daily actions, manners and speech are reflected, affords many a life story of romance, sorrow or success. Then there is, if it be one's first experience, all the charm of novelty in the life on board, and in noting the ever changing, but never uninteresting aspect of sky and ocean. The first day was spent thus although Holmes was content to spend his time in his cabin. While I was dressing for dinner Holmes rapped on my door and informed me that we were invited to dine at the captain's table, an honour indeed. I proceeded to take special care with my toilet before declaring myself ready.

On entering the state-room we were escorted to the table by a steward whose outfit was crisp and pristine and whose manner was politeness itself. The tables were laid extravagantly with napkins twisted into almost grotesque shapes and laid either by the plates or in the wine glasses which sparkled like the finest diamonds. All the tables had centre-pieces sculpted in various figures, towers, pyramids and the like. The material they had been fashioned from puzzled me momentarily until I realised upon closer inspection they were actually fashioned from brown macaroon paste. A sign of delights to come later.

The captain, Friedrich Moltke was a rather small man with undistinguished features who immediately put me in mind of Inspector Lestrade. He was content to let the conversation flow around him whilst he remained its calm centre. The conversation covered many subjects, all of them discussed in convivial fashion. Our fellow guests at the table were two American couples, the Browns and the Robesons. Introductions were made all round. Richard Brown and his wife Agatha hailed from Hoboken in the state of New Jersey where Richard Brown was a noted lawyer and Agatha an equally noted teacher of mathematics. The Robesons were domiciled in Fall River, Massachusetts. Both husband and wife worked side by side in the running of the American Print Company, the largest such company in Fall River they assured us, employing upward of six thousand people in their huge mill.

"Fall River is at the forefront of textile printing, we are known far and wide for it and I am mighty proud to be able to carry on the good work of my forebears. My namesake set up the very first such print work back in 1824 folks. Yes sir, when people think of Fall River they think of textile printing," crowed Andrew Robeson.

"I am sure you are correct in what you say, particularly for those who are in some way connected with the industry you champion, but I think in general there will be those people whose only knowledge of Fall River is the infamous incident involving the Borden family. Although my friend Watson here is not particularly well versed in sensational crimes, I am confident even he will know of this case."

"I do, although I am tolerably confident that I do not recall it in such detail as you, Holmes. I remember being particularly horrified at the thought a daughter could inflict such injuries on her father and mother. With an axe was it not?"

"More likely a hatchet although the distinction is not great and you are mistaken in thinking it was her mother who was one of the victims, it was actually her stepmother."

"She was exonerated I recall."

"Yes, she was acquitted. I know very little of her life after that although I feel sure Mr Robeson could enlighten us."

"To be honest, Mr Holmes none of us in Fall River like to dwell for too long on that episode. It gave the town a certain notoriety we could have done without and the Borden family were very well respected, they are synonymous with the textile industry of our town. But to answer your question, sir, Lizzie Borden still resides in the town and lives with her sister Emma in a house they bought after their inheritance came through. But, sir, whilst Emma is tolerated in society, her sister is not."

I felt more than a little indignant on this woman's behalf for she had been tried and adjudged not guilty. There seemed to be no good reason for such ostracism.

"But she was acquitted Mr Robeson, hasn't she been through enough without Fall River society shunning her?" I asked heatedly.

"She was acquitted, you are quite correct Doctor, no one, but no one in Fall River believes her to be innocent. She is as guilty as hell, excuse my language, ladies."

After that emphatic response from Andrew Robeson, the conversation was steered back to calmer waters and lighter topics. So absolutely motionless was the steamer during the two hours of feasting and bonhomie it seemed scarcely credible that we were speeding across the Atlantic Ocean at a rate approaching fifteen knots. There were sounds of gaiety from the deck where some form of dancing was obviously taking place.

On taking the air for a promenade I found the upper deck to be brightly illuminated with a surprising number of people still abroad, considering the lateness of the hour, dancing reels and the like. I declined any number of invitations to join in the festivities and set off on my promenade.

I returned to my cabin, more than ready to fall into the welcome arms of Morpheus and my last fleeting thought before slumber embraced me was of Lizzie Borden. I may have given her more than a fleeting thought if I had known how that particular crime would play a part in our six months tenure in New York.

Ellis Island

Chapter Three

The next few days of the voyage progressed very much along the lines of the pattern of the first day. I invariably rose late, as did Holmes and we usually strolled around the deck in the morning, if for nothing else then to raise an appetite for luncheon although I abstained from that particular meal for the final three days before our arrival in New York, deciding that the generous breakfast provided would quite easily see me through to the evening dinner. Other than that, I visited the well-stocked library and thumbed through a whole range of magazines and periodicals. Holmes sometimes accompanied me, but more often than not he was to be found in his cabin, preparing himself for his new charges.

As porters saw to our trunks in readiness to disembark, we went up on to the deck. The first thing that caught our eye was a huge conflagration with smoke billowing over the city in a large plume.

"Ellis Island," said Holmes, "the United States Immigration Station is on the island and it looks as though the main building is the one ablaze."

"Lord help anyone out there."

"Indeed, Watson. It's not unusual to have upwards of six hundred immigrants there on any given day."

My attention eventually turned to the skyline of the city. As far as my eyes could see the city was stretching towards the sky. Even on this slow approach to the port I could recognise this was a city teeming with life, humming with trade and muttering with the thunder of passage. The city seemed so vast as to be an endless world, an endless world of possibilities where hopes, dreams and ambitions could be realised.

The class barriers which were so evident on board the SS *Bremen* were no less strictly enforced when we docked and disembarked. The third-class passengers were inspected and vetted before being herded into vast iron-clad halls or borne away to Ellis Island for further interrogation where I suspected normality would rule despite the recent blaze. Eventually these immigrants, like ourselves, would be allowed to tread the broad avenues and streets of this New World.

We disembarked and were caught up in the surge of first class and second class passengers being driven toward the arrivals hall where there was more vetting being carried out. At length it was decided that we were, if not eminently desirable, then at least acceptable and in no time at all we found ourselves out in the sunshine of the morning scanning the horizon for Wilson Hargreave who was due to be meeting us.

Small, scruffy looking lads who looked as though they were in need of a square meal, beseeching the waiting folk to buy the newspapers they were attempting to thrust into everyone's arms with various degrees of success. *The New York Herald, The New York World, The New York Journal* and *The New York Press* were prominent amongst these. They were all on sale for three American cents each and Holmes scooped up an armful as he threw coins in all directions.

We were approached by a fresh-faced, youthful looking fellow who was dressed in a long black overcoat despite the clement weather. He was carrying a large sheet of paper which had Holmes's name written on it in large block capital letters. Holmes stepped forward.

"I am Sherlock Holmes," he announced and this is my friend and colleague, Doctor Watson."

"James O' Connell, New York Police Bureau. Wilson is kinda tied up just now and by rights I should be with him, but he needed a nursemaid so here I am, no offence folks."

He studied me intensely for a few moments.

"Wilson thought you might bring a lady friend with you," he said, addressing Holmes.

"The fair sex is Watson's department, O' Connell. My interests lie elsewhere."

The colour drained from O' Connell's face. "You don't mean…"

"No, I do not mean *that!*"

I let out an involuntary chuckle at Holmes's momentary discomfort as I stepped up into the cab that O'Connell had waiting for us. Holmes followed and we settled down upon the fine upholstered seats.

"The Belle Vue hotel, Park Avenue South please, driver," shouted O'Connell. "Gramercy Park, gents," he explained to us, "the department has turned an old store into a training school to find the next breed of detectives to take us over from the many aging ones. As I understand it, Mr Holmes that's where you come in although personally I find it peculiar that we can't find work for home-grown detectives who can pass their knowledge and experience on. No offence, Mr Holmes, it's just an observation on my part."

"No offence taken, your views are no doubt shared by others, but I am confident that I will not be carrying this burden alone and home-grown detectives will feature strongly. Besides, my work here will be done in six months and I will be more than happy to pass the baton to others who will continue to encourage and instruct future generations of detectives."

O'Connell appeared to be satisfied with this answer and voiced no further opinion on the matter. Holmes fell into a brown study and I took the time to study the city as it flashed by as the cab raced through the streets with a driver who charged past every obstacle in his way with no deviation of direction or lessening of pace. The broad thoroughfares were almost impossibly full of noise as the people flooded the streets going about their business. A cacophony of sound that was unknown to me, for London although a bustling, busy city could not hold a candle to the sights and sounds I experienced in our mad flight from the port to Gramercy Park that day. The city was a startling apparition fashioned from steel and stone, a living entity it seemed and one that fed off its population; an unstoppable juggernaut bent on domination.

The Belle Vue was a hotel of middling size, but was clean, bright and very welcoming as was the management; a husband and wife team, Mr and Mrs Kuhns. Frank Kuhns was a tall, bespectacled man who towered over his wife, Lavinia. He had a pronounced stoop, no doubt from spending most of his waking day bending forward to listen to the views of his wife who was garrulous in the extreme and kept up a never-ending stream of dialogue about family members and incidents we obviously had no knowledge of. Billy, the bell-boy, a slight young man, carried our bags to the fourth floor where we were pleased to find two very well appointed rooms each with their own bathroom and a separate study.

O' Connell waited for us in the dining-room where a beautifully embroidered sign set out the etiquette required for dining in the Belle Vue: NO BELCHING NO SPITTING. I shuddered to think what manner of guests would require that this be pointed out to them.

"Now, gents, Wilson is hoping to meet you tomorrow morning at nine-thirty to escort you to the new school and introduce you to the principal, Eugene Seitz. If he is still tied up trying to crack this latest murder, then you may expect to see me again although Lord knows I would prefer to be doing some proper police work. No offence, folks."

"None taken," sighed Holmes. "This latest murder as you term it, is it a simple affair?"

"Simple enough Mr Holmes, a domestic affair. All Wilson needs is a confession and he will have cracked it."

"Latest murder you say, how many have there been this year?" I asked.

"By my reckoning it's around fifty to sixty."

"Fifty to sixty!" I exclaimed sharply. "I was not expecting a figure like that."

"You're in America now," said Holmes light-heartedly. "And believe it or not Watson, the murder rate for New York is somewhat lower than that of some other cities."

"I'll leave you folks to it then, Frank and Lavinia will look after you just fine. Goodbye."

O' Connell took his leave and sauntered off on foot, the cab driver having decided not to wait in spite of instruction to the contrary.

"Have you been to New York before, gentlemen?" asked Lavinia Kuhns and not waiting for a reply, steamed on. "London isn't it, you are from? My cousin Elizabeth went there last year, she wasn't impressed. That is my Aunt Isadora's girl you know. That's my mother's sister, Elizabeth's mother and wouldn't you just know it, my father's sister is also an Elizabeth although most folk call her Eliza. She is living in Buffalo, Elizabeth, I mean not Eliza, well I mean her mother lives in Buffalo too, Isadora of course, who met her husband when he was clearing snow outside the school she was at. Not that she was a teacher, although she is now, no, gents she was a pupil and fell in love hard with James her husband. Of course it was a few years before they wed, she was only fifteen when they met after all, but James was content to wait. My mother said it wouldn't last, but she said the same about Frank and me and look how happy we are after all these years, eh Frank?"

Frank Kuhns nodded and in that instant Holmes was at the door ready to make good our escape.

"What say, Watson we take a turn around the park?"

"An excellent idea, Holmes."

"If you should need a guide, I have nothing particularly pressing on me for an hour or two…" offered Mr Kuhns.

He was silenced by a, "But, Frank…" from his wife and he nodded resignedly with a sigh.

Mrs Kuhns followed us out into the hall and picked up a bunch of keys from underneath the reception desk.

"You will be needing one of these," she said, handing a large ornate key to Holmes. "Take care with it, we only have the two."

"Is it not a public park, Mrs Kuhns?" I asked.

"No, it has never been open to the public. Local residents and some businesses in close proximity to the park are allowed two keys each to the park gates."

"Never fear, dear lady, we will take the greatest of care of the key and return it to you forthwith."

As we walked in the small yet beautiful park, Holmes discussed his fears and hopes with regard to his temporary post.

"In spite of my earlier enthusiasm for this American venture of mine, I cannot help, but feel like a fish out of water. Are my methods too dated for this modern city with its modern brand of detective?"

"I certainly don't believe that to be the case, Holmes, nor would Scotland Yard or the criminal classes of Europe. Your methods will be just as effective here as they have been anywhere."

"We must wish then that my students will see it that way."

"It's quite an undertaking, how will you proceed?"

"That rather depends on the calibre of the students and their willingness to learn. If they have no thirst for knowledge then I will have to impress upon them the need for such knowledge. If they possess no moral compass then I will have to set them on the right path. The New York Police Bureau has been bedevilled by corruption for many years in spite of periodical purges to root out those who are guilty of such corruption. Tomorrow will give us a firm idea of all of that of course."

"If I can be of any help at all, Holmes, please be assured I will do all I can."

"I would certainly be grateful for your company tomorrow my dear fellow."

"Then you shall have it."

Although I was more than willing to assist Holmes in any way I possibly could and indeed was pleased that he perceived me of being some use in his endeavours, I was doubtful that I could be of any real assistance to him in his new role. I pride myself on being an intelligent man, but often found myself lacking when compared to the kind of rarefied intellect as displayed so often by my friend.

Mrs Kuhns waylaid us as we entered the hotel and our simple inquiry as to what time we may expect dinner to be served was met with a lengthy, detailed and rather tiresome story involving her paternal grandfather and a business trip to Illinois. Good manners prevented me from doing anything other than nodding and smiling politely as the tale unfolded. These rules of etiquette, however, did not prevent Holmes from excusing himself and ascending the stairs to his room. Mrs Kuhns, barely pausing for breath, was not aware of his absence until her tale was told and her annoyance was only visible through a slight grimace and an almost imperceptible shake of her head.

Dinner was in fact to be served at seven pm sharp, a fact I apprised Holmes of before settling down for a welcome nap. The nap turned into a deep slumber, being only awakened by Holmes shaking my shoulder. For an instant I imagined myself back in Baker Street with Holmes crying 'the game is afoot' before we rushed out into the gas lit street, but this waking dream dissipated and I realised that temporarily at least, New York was our home.

The meal was simple enough fare; imagination in the cuisine was replaced by heartiness and plain good old-fashioned nourishment, I for one was not complaining. The wine was a Californian burgundy and was very fine indeed. The evening meal was by no means a formal occasion, fellow guests wandered in and out of the dining-room as and when they chose, they sat; they stood and generally behaved as though they were in a tavern. We did however converse freely with those of the guests we introduced ourselves to. The Belle Vue seemed to cater for visitors who came to the city on business for as far as we could ascertain none of those assembled were in New York on vacation. Strictly speaking, this was not a holiday for Holmes although it could be construed as one for me. Holmes retired at a quite early hour having scarcely touched his burgundy. I smoked a final pipe of the day before bringing my first day in New York to a close with a few words of wisdom from Mrs Kuhns regarding the perils of smoking tobacco just before retiring. Needless to say, this involved a cautionary tale featuring many of her family members.

The Belle Vue Hotel

James O' Connell

Chapter Four

I was somewhat apprehensive regarding what fare would be on offer for breakfast. I was not naïve enough to think that Mrs Kuhns would be duplicating what we would expect to eat on the other side of the Atlantic Ocean, but I hoped it would approximate to something I was fairly familiar with.

On a long dresser against the wall there were various offerings laid out such as fruit, milk and hard boiled eggs which fell short by some way of my food of choice for a morning meal. I was intrigued by some pillow-shaped biscuits, which to me had the appearance of a tightly-formed besom. They were firm to the touch and looked distinctly unappetising, but as I brought one to my mouth to try, Mrs Kuhns nudged me.

"They are eaten with milk, Doctor Watson, pop a couple into a bowl there and pour the milk over them. They will soften up a treat. Some folk sprinkle sugar over them, but to my mind they taste better without; more natural like."

"What actually is it though, Mrs Kuhns?"

"It's just wheat pure and simple."

I reasoned it must be an acquired taste as I attempted to chew my way through one of the biscuits and definitely a taste I could not see myself acquiring. I sprinkled some sugar over the top of the other biscuit in my bowl, but this failed to make the whole experience any more pleasant. The aroma of bacon and eggs from the kitchen I decided was much more to my liking.

When Holmes appeared a few minutes later he was content to drink coffee only. I had always found that Holmes, at breakfast, was either completely ravenous or would abstain altogether. Outwardly he appeared without a care and entirely confident, yet without coming anywhere close to Holmes's deductive skills I was able to glimpse a certain amount of nervousness behind the calm exterior he presented to the world on this particular morning.

"Do not worry yourself too much, Holmes, I am sure today will go very well for you."

"Worry, Watson? Do I appear worried?"

"Not to the untrained eye, no," I chuckled. "There are certain signs present which lead me to my conclusion."

"Well, well, perhaps the art of detection is contagious after all, my dear fellow. Perhaps you will be good enough to explain your chain of reasoning?"

"Certainly, Holmes. You have quite obviously rushed your toilet this morning, this much is by apparent by your collar. I am of the opinion that you would have endeavoured to be fastidious regarding your appearance today so that fact plus my observation that you have nicked yourself in two places whilst shaving speak to me of a certain apprehension as to how you will acquit yourself today."

"Excellent, Watson."

"Elementary," said I.

Mrs Kuhns bustled by, replenishing our coffee cups and making sure we were happy with the breakfast fare.

"Oh, Mr Holmes, you have cut yourself," she said, dabbing the corner of her less than pristine apron on Holmes's neck. "My father was a one for that, gents. Of course, that was in his later years when, between you and me, he had lost his marbles completely. My mother would lose patience with him and it was left to me and my siblings to look after him as best we could. Not that my brother, William was any use to us. A shirker, he was, a shirker. If he could add to our burden he would. He is still like it today; his daughter could tell you many tales that would break your heart. Family is family though and we do stick together, even my cousin Theodore who was the black sheep of the family, he was plenty mischievous as a child and my mother was heard to say many times that he would end up in jail and that is exactly what happened owing to his holding up a liquor store in Boston. Still, we can't choose our family can we?"

"No," offered Holmes, "nor one's landladies in life."

Following a sharp tapping on the door, Mrs Kuhns ushered in the familiar figure of James O' Connell. It appeared to be a perfectly warm day yet once again he was in an overcoat buttoned up to the neck.

"Good morning, gents. I trust I am not too early," he said, looking at the coffee cups in front of us.

"Your punctuality is to be commended," said Holmes, "as opposed to our tardiness. No Hargreave?"

"Wilson has an arrest to make this morning so I have been taken from other duties, detective duties you know, to accompany you. No offence," he replied.

"Most assuredly, none taken," said Holmes, without wholly succeeding in keeping a note of exasperation out of his voice. "Help yourself to a cup of Mrs Kuhns's most excellent coffee and we will be with you shortly."

I only needed a few moments before declaring myself ready for whatever the day would throw at me. Holmes was a few minutes longer before reappearing with a sheaf of notes under his arms.

"The fruits of my labours," he said, patting the bundle affectionately. "Ripe and ready to be passed on."

O'Connell was waiting impatiently in the vestibule, drumming his fingers on the table. "If you are finally ready, gents, please follow me."

There was no cab waiting outside for it was a walk of just a few minutes to our destination. The building the New York Police Bureau had purchased to house their new college in was a former department store, much larger than anything I had ever encountered before. The shoppers who thronged Gamages would have professed themselves amazed at the sheer scope and size of this former temple to Mammon and the spending of it. The department store in question had moved into premises in Manhattan which I was assured by O'Connell was even more stupendous. Once inside we could see, as O' Connell took us on a tour of the building, that it had been sub-divided into sections which housed, not just classrooms, but a pistol firing range, a gymnasium, a canteen and an element which certainly pleased Holmes, a library. I felt more than a little proud to notice the library contained in a division marked 'SHERLOCK HOLMES', some of my own humble efforts. I pointed out to Holmes before he could comment on the jarring juxtaposition of my chronicles with these casebooks of crime, copies of his monographs on various aspects of crime detection.

"I had not been consulted," he said, "but all the same, it is rather pleasing."

O'Connell followed Holmes's gaze with a look of ennui on his face.

"I daresay there will be not much call for your monographs in this modern city of ours, Mr Holmes. Police work is rather more physical here and fancy theories have no place in this city. No offence, Mr Holmes."

"Well, who knows, you may yet prove to be right and I assure you O'Connell if I was in the habit of taking offence at your statements then you may be assured I would have done so already and incidentally, you would be the first to know."

"Just so long as you know that I will always be straight with you whether you like it or not, it's the kind of man I am," replied O'Connell. "If you are ready, gents, I'll take you to Eugene Seitz; don't want him getting all hornery on us. He is not the most patient of men."

O' Connell's statement was an exercise in understatement for Mr Seitz, when we were introduced to him in his office was fairly apoplectic in his own impatience with our perceived tardiness. He was a slight man with whiskers that belonged to a bygone age and a manner to suit.

"Perhaps it is the custom to keep people waiting in England, but I can assure it is not so here. I do not tolerate it from the students under my care nor will I tolerate it from my staff however distinguished they think they are."

"My dear sir," said Holmes, "A thousand apologies, I fear we tarried too long admiring the excellent facilities you have here. I have no doubt that you yourself are responsible in no small way for these. I was not sure what to expect, but now I see that I will look forward immensely to working under a guiding light such as yourself."

Holmes did not exactly wink at me as he addressed Seitz, for it was an action I had never seen him perform, but he came as close to it that day as I had ever seen. Taking my cue from my friend, I mumbled my own apologies, insincere though they may have been and Eugene Seitz instantly calmed down. He was just as susceptible to flattery as Holmes himself.

"I fear I must offer my apologies too, gentlemen. I may be a little worked up today. I am normally the calmest of men."

A distinct cough from O'Connell behind us, greeted this statement.

Seitz continued on, "I am pleased, Mr Holmes, that you admire the facilities on offer here, I have worked hard to that end and I can quite rightly say that I am proud of what we have achieved so far and I am confident that this seat of learning will help produce the finest police force in the world."

He went on to explain that this academy as he called it would not only result in the finest and ablest detectives of any police force, but would also educate the humble policemen on the beat to be the most comprehensively trained of any such 'foot-soldiers' anywhere. They were drilled in self-defence, un-armed combat down to more mundane skills such as simple map-reading. In the basement a rifle/pistol range had been installed where all students no matter where their ultimate destination in the NYPB would be, were taught the basic skills of discharging their weapons safely. Moral guidance had not been overlooked either. There had been too many instances of corruption within the force for this aspect of being an officer to be overlooked. During this resumé of the academy's aims the irascible Eugene Seitz had been replaced by a committed, conscientious and inordinately proud man.

It was now time for Holmes to meet his students, one of whom Seitz expected to take up the reins of tutorship after Holmes had departed these shores.

As Seitz invited us to follow him, O'Connell bade us goodbye. "Well, gents I will leave you in capable hands and I will return to proper detective work. No…"

"…offence? Yes, we know. Thank you for being the most ablest of nursemaids. Please give my regards to Hargreave. Goodbye," said Holmes.

Holmes had told me earlier that he was expected to have twenty pupils under his care initially who would be put through their paces during the next eleven weeks. There would then be a break of two weeks then another group of twenty students would be presented to Holmes. The highest achieving student from the first twenty would be chosen as Holmes's assistant for the second term. Quite understandably in my view, Holmes had expressed some disquiet regarding the ability of any one of his students attempting to take on the mantle of assistant after so short a time, but he was more than willing to go along with the scheme.

I was fully expecting to find a room full of fresh-faced youngsters so was somewhat surprised to find a mix of students who ranged from indeed fresh-faced youngsters to those who could only be described as grizzly veterans. I subsequently learnt that one or two of those veterans had been pounding the beat for upwards of twenty years and were eminently happy to be given this opportunity to advance themselves.

Eugene Seitz introduced Sherlock Holmes to the assembled students and took his leave.

"Good morning everyone, I trust you are all well. May I introduce to you my friend and colleague, Doctor Watson? As some of you are no doubt aware, Doctor Watson also acts as the chronicler of my adventures as he terms them and whilst he is prone to embellishments, he is a fairly faithful scribe and witness to the cases which come my way."

I added my own 'good morning' and hastily took my seat next to Holmes at the front of the room, still not knowing what, if anything, Holmes was requiring from me.

"Now," continued Holmes, "we will begin by considering the essential skills that are required by any successful detective, but first, please stand up and identify yourselves to me, the good doctor and your fellow students."

One by one, they rose and volunteered information about themselves. Most were content to just state their name and age; others gave us some idea of their aims, goals and ambitions. Holmes occasionally nodded during these comments, but did not interrupt with any remarks of his own. When all twenty had said their piece, Holmes got to his feet.

"Thank you, gentlemen. We have a long three months ahead of us, but for those amongst you who are the most committed it may possibly be the most informative three months of your lives. Although, I do not mean to necessarily imply that all of you will fail to graduate, success is, of course, dependent on your application, attitude and willingness to embrace all I can impart to you. Now before we discuss the essential tools of our trade, I have twenty copies of our schedule for the coming months which friend Watson, will distribute amongst you. If you would be so kind, Watson?"

"Certainly, Holmes," I replied with a strained smile, having not thought of my role as that of a lackey. The timetable printed on the leaflet was crowded with lectures full of Holmes's specialist knowledge; cigar ash, footprints, tattoos, hand-writing to name but a few.

"Occasionally," continued Holmes, "I have had reason to admonish the good doctor on his failure to both look and observe, but even so as he knows me so well, better than anybody, I might add, I feel sure he will be glad to give you the three essential qualities that I deem necessary for any detective."

"Observation, deduction and knowledge."

"The three foundation stones of our profession, gentlemen. Today we will concentrate our energies on them."

I excused myself, being none too sure that Holmes needed me in any useful capacity and went in search of a coffee, accepting the fact that a cup of tea may be out of the question. I located the small canteen area that we had strolled by earlier and ordered myself a coffee and an oddly shaped biscuit, springy to the touch and rather bland as it turned out. After assaulting my digestive system thus, I made my way to the library where I indulged myself in a volume or two of American homicides and sleep. Some little while later I stirred at the sound of Holmes's voice.

"And this is where knowledge can be gained, gentlemen. The present resonates with the echoes of the past and this is particularly true of crime. There is nothing new under the sun and you will find that the interplay of ideas combined with oblique uses of knowledge extraordinarily useful to you. This library is a veritable treasure trove of the great cases from around the world and I urge you all to take advantage of it. This room is a history of crime, a history we can all learn from. Education never ends. Have any of you had a previous opportunity to study particular cases? I see Watson here has been looking into the Lizzie Borden affair before sleep put an end to his studies."

One of the students spoke up. "Now, that is one case I have a particular interest in."

"And why might that be, Hogan?" asked Holmes.

"I am kin to the Bordens. It's a large and important family in Fall River. I always make a point of paying a call to Emma when I find myself back home."

"Emma being?"

"Lizzie's sister, Holmes."

"Why, thank you, Watson. I had momentarily forgotten. Pray, continue, Hogan."

"Well, that was it really, sir. Except to say that Emma would still, after these five years, like to know the truth of what happened that day. She is protective of her sister especially in view of the ostracism that Lizzie encounters."

"We heard a little of that during our voyage to these shores for we encountered members of another leading Fall River family; the Robesons."

"I don't suppose you would be prepared to look into the case on Emma's behalf would you, sir?"

"I very much fear my time in this country will be entirely taken up with tutoring you fine fellows."

"There is a two week break in between terms…"

"Hogan, I will give it some thought as it is certainly a case that intrigues me, but I am unable to make any promises at this time."

"Thank you."

I excused myself once more and set off for a stroll around Gramercy Park, collecting the key from Mrs Kuhns who managed to occupy fully thirty minutes of my time in the recounting of a family event from her seemingly unlimited 'archives'.

When I arrived back at the hotel Mrs Kuhns informed me I had a visitor; news that intrigued for I knew no one in this city. A tall distinguished looking man came into the lobby and introduced himself as Wilson Hargreave of the NYPB.

"Pleased to meet you. I'm afraid Holmes is still busy at the college."

"That will not be a problem, Doctor as it is you I have come to see. I have a proposition for you."

"Please continue."

"I'm sure you have plans of your own for your stay, but if I could impinge on them a little. We find ourselves two police surgeons short due to sudden bereavement and a domestic accident so my question is, would you like to help us out in our time of need? It will not be every day, some weeks we may not call on you at all so there will be ample time for sightseeing. What do you say, Doc?"

"I am none too sure my present level of medical knowledge is quite up to scratch enough for the kind of position you propose, but I would of course be glad to offer my assistance such as it may be."

"Thank you kindly. I have to dash now, but I will see call on you tomorrow around ten and we can iron out the details between us then."

"I will look forward to seeing you."

I informed Holmes of Hargreave's offer as we compared notes on our day. Holmes did not seem unduly surprised and I briefly wondered whether he and Hargreave had conspired together and this tale of injured and bereaved police surgeons had been concocted to give me something useful to do rather than get in Holmes's hair at the college. I thought of asking him directly, but I realised that approach would gain me nothing.

Eugene Seitz

The NYPB College

Chapter Five

My temporary position as a police surgeon within the NYPB began in the most gruesome fashion and almost immediately. Barely a week had gone by since Hargreave had filled me in a little on my duties when I received a wire at the hotel asking me to stand ready to be collected by cab and taken to a scene of a supposed homicide. A junior officer duly arrived in a cab and we were racing through the crowded streets in no time. The heat was stifling and the hardened New Yorkers who had regaled me with tales of hot summers in the city were now wishing the temperature would plummet. The whole city seemed to be full of tensions brought about by the stifling heat. Tempers were raised on every corner, cabmen screamed at each other to give way as bystanders looked on, bemused, but not in any way surprised.

The officer told me we were heading to the East River, to the area of East 11th Street Docks where children playing had spotted something in the water and fished it ashore only to get the shock of their lives.

"What was it? I am assuming it's a body."

"In a manner of speaking, yes."

"Meaning?"

"Just the upper torso and arms, Doctor."

We rode on in silence until we reached our destination, where there was quite a sizeable crowd of onlookers being held back by a single policeman.

O'Connell pushed his way through the throng to greet me. "I hope you have a strong stomach Doctor Watson for this kind of thing, I truly do. I have a notion you may be not up to the job. No offence, Doc."

"None taken, O'Connell. During my army service, I saw things on the plains of Afghanistan that would give you nightmares for the rest of your life, bodies torn asunder, limbs hacked and thrown around the battlefield like playthings, men so full of holes that they no longer resembled men. I think therefore, O'Connell, that I am up to the job."

"Well, I guess that told me. One up for you, Doc," he said, as he beckoned me to follow him.

Wilson Hargreave was standing over the upper torso and arms of a man. A powerful man he must have been in life, judging by his barrel-chest which now sported a peculiar injury whereby a strip of skin some four inches square had been excised. His arms were muscular indeed; I encircled my hand around his biceps and gave an involuntary whistle.

"Quite a man wasn't he?" said Hargreave. "Manual worker would you say?"

"It seems likely, Hargreave."

"We have had problems with medical students playing pranks in this area. Perhaps someone is having a laugh at our expense."

"I do not think so. The separation of the torso from the rest of the body is not the work of anyone in medical practice; the work is far too rudimentary."

"Unless it's what they want us to think."

Just then a messenger appeared who made straight for Hargreave and pressed a note into his hand. He glanced at the message, nodding his head.

"It seems we can re-unite our friend here with the rest of his body. There has been, shall we say, an interesting discovery in Harlem."

Hargreave gave instructions that the torso be removed to the Bellevue morgue along with the distinctive red and gold oilcloth it had been wrapped in. In the meantime, we set off for Harlem. There was a similar scene by the river bank when we arrived. A torso washed up would always, one presumes, be newsworthy and crowds automatically gravitate to such events.

That this, the lower torso and hips, belonged to the same man was evident. This part of the body had been wrapped in a piece of the same decorated oilcloth we had seen earlier. There was not much we could do at the scene so Hargreave suggested I be taken to the morgue to begin my preliminary investigation while he and his team started their onerous task of identifying this poor soul.

The morgue was a few blocks north of where we were, being situated in a squat brick building on Twenty-Sixth Street. It was a windowless building some sixty by eighty feet wide, lined along one side with marble slabs, the other with chest-high tiers of cooled body drawers. Up above there was a single skylight which did very little to alleviate the gloom of this understandably miserable place. I was surprised to find a complete absence of fans and the buzzing flies were an unwelcome distraction. Water dripped everywhere, water was directed at the bodies in a thin stream to try and preserve at least some freshness while necessary work was carried out. There must have been at least twenty bodies laid out on the rows of slabs. I had never seen anything quite like it.

An attendant greeted me.

"You must be Doctor Watson, I am Calvin Marcum. I can't help thinking you are wasting your time here," he said, gesturing towards the torso, which was incongruously sitting up on one the slabs.

"Why do you think that?"

"Medical students. Bane of our lives. This feller probably came from here in the first place. Look, all we need to do is tag him, bag him and if no one claims him, there is a potter's field which will accommodate him well enough out there on Hart Island."

"I am not so sure, but when the rest of the body arrives we will have a much better idea of what has occurred here."

There was some commotion out in the corridor, a few raised voices.

"Whatever is going on out there?"

Marcum shrugged his shoulders. "Nothing new there, it's the reporters doing their rounds, sniffing out a story or two. They turn up here every day at the same time, regular as clockwork."

I turned my attention to the mortal remains in front of me. The wound on the chest puzzled me, although a stab to the heart was the undoubted cause of death. Was the tearing away of the skin a deliberate action by someone or an accident, although I could not conceive of any accident to account for it? There were no obvious wounds on the arms and nothing on his hands to suggest that he had tried to defend himself. While I was carrying out the examination, Marcum just shook his head and repeated his words of earlier.

"You're wasting your time, just plumb wasting it."

More commotion outside of the room heralded the arrival of the lower torso of the unfortunate victim. It was carried into the room, wrapped in another piece of oilcloth, by a rather pale-faced policeman. He was very relieved to hand over both his burden and responsibility to me.

"The Captain asked me to tell you that the legs may be arriving shortly, some have been found down by the Brooklyn naval yard."

"Thank you, that will be all, unless you want to try and keep those reporters out there in some kind of order."

I was joined by a gentleman who suddenly appeared from a side-door. He introduced himself to me as Doctor Thomas Murphy, the superintendent of the mortuary, but his view of the matter was similar to Marcum's.

"Medical students up to their tricks again, eh?"

"I do not think so," I replied, pointing out the entrance wound on the chest. "It is quite deliberate and would undoubtedly have been fatal," I added.

Murphy peered at the upper torso intently. "Well, keep up the good work. I must go and have a word with the gentlemen of the press although I use the word 'gentlemen' with a great deal of caution and misgiving."

Having established the cause of death I proceeded to look for clues as to his identity. It was a fruitless task, there were no distinguishing marks or tattoos, no clues as to his trade although I was tolerably confident Holmes would have been able to find some small thing that would set him on the track. With that in mind I would suggest to Hargreave that we involve Holmes's help. I made a note of an abscessed finger which I reasoned may assist with identification.

It must have been well over an hour later when Hargreave arrived and I had no need to request Holmes's assistance for he accompanied Hargreave into the morgue. The legs, no longer missing, were wheeled in on a gurney. Of the head, there was still no sign.

Holmes paced around the slab on which the body parts had been assembled like an almost complete human jigsaw. From time to time he would come to a stop and peer intently at the body and mutter inaudibly. He picked the arms, each in turn, and made a particular examination of the hands and fingers, running his own index finger over the abscessed finger of the victim.

"Interesting," he remarked.

"Have you found something, Holmes?"

"Nothing beyond the obvious, no."

"The obvious being that we have a dead body we cannot identify nor do we know anything about this man's life," said O'Connell.

"Oh, I think we can do a little better than that. Once we have established his profession, his identity will surely follow."

"I don't see how we can possibly come up with a profession or trade for him. I would take a stab that given his size and apparent strength that he was a manual worker and given where the body parts appeared, possibly a dock worker. It's a transitory type of work and men come and go as they please, but we may be able to sniff out one of their number who has gone missing. Pity we have no tattoos or the like to help nudge people's memories," said Hargreave.

"The tattoo on the chest may just do that, if..."

"But there is no tattoo," I said.

"Indeed, no, Watson, but that strip of skin has been torn away for a reason, don't you think? And what better reason than to remove some distinctive feature such as a tattoo?"

"That might be so, but it would be of more darn use if we knew what kind of tattoo, but I don't suppose for one moment you can tell us that can you?" O'Connell asked with a sneer.

"Oh, I think I may be able to enlighten you. Momentarily I thought it was a woman's name, but just as quickly dismissed the notion as it is apparent to me that it must have been the image of a woman, a portrait if you like."

"How can you possibly know that?"

"The location tells us the tattoo will be of something close to this man's heart both figuratively and literally. A name does not fit the bill, you only have to imagine how it would appear in a mirror, but an image picked out in ink, now that's different altogether. A wife, a first love, his mother even, but there we enter into the realm of conjecture."

"Excellent, Mr Holmes, that gives us something to work on. I will dispatch as many men as I can spare to go to the docks in search of a missing man with a tattooed chest."

"A sound plan, Hargreave, but with one flaw," said Holmes.

"Oh and what might that be?"

"Your men would be better employed visiting the Turkish baths and massage parlours of this city although I think we can concentrate on the areas running alongside the East river."

"Turkish bath, massage parlours? You are surely joking," exclaimed O'Connell. He turned to Hargreave, "this is going too far, this guy will have us running fool's errands. No offence, Mr Holmes."

By way of response, Holmes picked up the victim's left hand. "Have a good look, gentleman." He did the same with the right hand. "Once more, please study carefully."

"There is the abscessed finger Holmes, but nothing else that I can see."

"Then do not use your eyes alone, but run your fingers over his hand. Yes, just like that, Watson. Any thoughts?"

"Why, yes, his hands seem extraordinarily smooth."

"Indeed, so our 'dock worker' recedes into the background, but in his place we have a masseur for what other profession would result in the smooth hands we see, save for that of a 'rubber'."

"Ingenious, Mr Holmes," gushed Hargreave.

"Elementary, Hargreave."

Hargreave barked out a few orders to O'Connell who turned on his heel and left.

Holmes, in the meantime, was examining the oilcloth, turning the remnants over and over, sniffing the fabric as he did so. He picked up the cord which had been used to secure these grotesque bundles of flesh. "Window sash cord," he muttered. "The oilcloth may bear some fruit, it is rather distinctive. Still, we may have no need to follow that particular route."

There was nothing more we could do without more data coming to light so we made our way back to the hotel in a police growler. I, for one, was glad to be out of that damp, depressing building. As we arrived at the hotel I was forcibly struck by the incongruity of the hotel and morgue sharing the same name. I had made no plans for the weekend that now beckoned; being on call with the NYPB, although undeniably exciting had certainly curtailed various sight-seeing trips I had been looking forward to. Still, there was still the best part of six months to go and I was reasonably confident that my connection to the Bureau would come to an end within a few weeks.

Wilson Hargreave

Chapter Six

The following morning, Hargreave called upon us just as we were finishing the breakfast Mrs Kuhns had prepared and was now clearing away the remnants of whilst regaling us with a tale of a distant cousin in Wisconsin who once owned the biggest ranch in that state or it may have been the second-largest, I cannot quite recall.

"Drink it was, gentlemen, that's what drove him to his ruin, the love of good liquor. And just look at him now, sweeping the floor in a grocery store. There should be a law against it."

"Surely, Mrs Kuhns, a little drink in moderation has never done any harm and speaking as a medical man, it may even prove to be beneficial."

"Beneficial? Beneficial? I disagree. Beneficial indeed. Neither Frank nor me ever allow a drop to pass our lips do we?"

Frank Kuhns had entered the dining room as his wife made this statement. He nodded at her in such a way that suggested to me that the occasional drop did pass his lips! Hargreave brought a chair over to the table, waved Mrs Kuhns away and settled into his seat.

"We have a name to put to our face. Well, of course we have no face, but you know what I mean. Late last night two of my men made inquiries at the Murray Hill Turkish Baths on East 42nd Street. They learned that one of their rubbers failed to turn up for work some days ago and has made no contact since. He is a William Guldensuppe, a Dutchman, and how about this Mr Holmes, he had an abscessed finger and a tattoo on his chest of an old sweetheart."

"Excellent work, Hargreave. I have no doubt it will turn out to be a tiresome domestic incident which is destined only to be remembered by the extraordinary manner of the disposal of his corpse."

"We have his address; it's a small rooming-house on 9th Avenue. I thought you might care to join me, Mr Holmes as we could have been going round in circles had it not been for your assistance."

"What say you, Watson? Shall we give up some of our Saturday in a worthy cause?"

"I have nothing planned whatsoever, Holmes so if I can be of any help I'm your man."

"Excellent. Well, Hargreave you have your posse. If you will be patient with us, we will join you in a few minutes."

We clambered aboard the police vehicle with and the patiently waiting driver gave rein to the horses. The Saturday morning traffic was in full flow and I more than once idly wondered where everyone was going. The ride was punctuated by the driver's earthy comments and complaints which he directed at all and sundry who he perceived had placed obstacles in his way.

The rooming-house was an unprepossessing enough building, but no worse or better than similar properties on 9th Avenue and in some respects was in better condition than those we had just seen on neighbouring 34th Street, which Hargreave assured us had a much better reputation. A detective and two patrolmen were waiting outside. Rapping at the door brought forth a rather plump woman who informed us she was the landlady, a Mrs Augusta Nack.

"Is there a Mr Nack?" asked Hargreave.

"No, well there is, but he ain't here. He shipped out months back. Used to deliver bread, but he couldn't get his dough to rise if you know what I mean so he was no more use to me."

I was puzzled by Mrs Nack's accent as she ushered us inside. German, I wondered? Holmes, as so often, read my mind and whispered, "Danish," as we crossed the threshold.

"What's this all about?" she demanded.

"We are making enquiries regarding a William Guldensuppe, he is a tenant here we believe," stated Hargreave.

"He has shipped out too. Owes me money. Just cos I am a landlady don't mean I got money."

"Yet you seem to be contemplating a trip; your travel trunk there has had its locks oiled very recently, the drips on the fabric are still apparent you see and its appearance suggests to me that it is full. Let's see shall we…"

"That's private property, you have no right," she protested as Holmes flung back the lid to reveal a trunkful of clothes.

"Planning a trip I see," remarked Holmes.

"What of it?"

"You just protested to us of your lack of money, but the packed trunk and the unsightly bulge, which is apparent to me under your corset, is no doubt a bundle of a few hundred dollars. I think escape is on your mind, the question is why?"

"I can do what I like, mister."

"If doing what you like entails murder than I beg to be contrary."

"Murder, what do you mean, murder?"

Holmes nodded towards the corner of the room where there was a folded piece of oilcloth with a pattern which was only too familiar to us. Mrs Nack followed Holmes's gaze and visibly blanched.

"The game is up, but you can do yourself some good by telling us who you acted with as most assuredly you did not commit this act alone."

Mrs Nack mulled this over and after wrestling with her conscience decided on self-preservation if at all possible. She came up with the name Martin Thorn, a tenant and also a rival for her affections along with Guldensuppe. She claimed that Thorn had gone away with Guldensuppe last weekend and there, in a fit of jealous rage had despatched the Dutchman to his Maker. She only had knowledge of this when Thorn returned alone. Once he had confessed, she was in fear of her life hence her attempt at flight.

"Thank you, Mrs Nack. You statement is clear, concise and I would imagine bears very little resemblance to the truth. Hargreave, perhaps you would do the honours…"

"Certainly," he replied, coming forward and fixing the handcuffs around a protesting Mrs Nack's wrists.

Two days later, Thorn was arrested as he tried to cross the border into Canada. He denied all knowledge of the crime, but the evidence mounted up and a further confession by Mrs Nack, which detailed her own physical involvement in the murder, meant that both Thorn and Nack were charged with Guldensuppe's murder.

Holmes never spoke of the case again, it had none of those singular features that pique his interest so, save for the manner of disposing of the body and of course, he made clear from the outset, he was of the mind it would turn out to be a grubby, domestic incident.

Over the coming weeks my involvement with the NYPB lessened considerably, other perhaps better-qualified medical men who had been waiting in the wings now pressed their claims to be part of the team. I was not unduly unhappy at this turn of events for we were nearly half way through our six month tenure in the city and with a two week break fast approaching I hoped Holmes would join me in a little travelling, the schedule of which I was busy working on. As often with Sherlock Holmes, events conspired against us and our destination was to be Fall River, Massachusetts.

Fall River Line. Pier 14 New York

Chapter Seven

"I have been giving some thought to young Hogan's suggestion, Watson," announced Holmes as we breakfasted together one morning shortly before the end of Holmes's first term.

"You'll have to enlighten me as to his suggestion. I know from previous comments of yours that he is shaping up well and he will make make a fine detective and also the fact he will be your 'lieutenant' for the next term, but I cannot recall a suggestion of his."

"Well, it was some three months ago, Watson, so I suppose I cannot blame you for forgetting. Hogan is kin to the Borden family of Fall River and was desirous that I travel to that town and look into the savage murders of Andrew Borden and his wife, Abby. If you recall, Lizzie Borden was charged with the murders, but acquitted although the fingers still point at her. Hogan, more than anything, would like me to put Emma Borden's, Lizzie's sister, mind at rest as regards her sister's innocence."

"All that is very well I am sure, but why go further into it, what have you got to gain?"

"What, indeed? It is art for art's sake, Watson."

"What of the Fall River police force? One hardly expects that they will welcome a stranger in their midst raking over the coals of a case that presumably remains officially unsolved."

"Ordinarily, I would say you have a point, but as Hogan's uncle is chief of police in Fall River we may find ourselves unhindered in our quest."

"You wish me to accompany you?"

"If you would be so kind, Watson, a trusty comrade and friend is always of use."

"Then, I am your man."

"Good old Watson!"

"When do we depart?"

"In five days' time. Lodgings have been arranged for us at a house next door to the murder house."

"Very well. Fall River it is."

I attended the college on the final day of the term, when diplomas were handed out to all those who had taken part. Holmes was pleased that all twenty students had completed the course, admittedly with varying degrees of success. Hogan and an Irish-American, McMullen were adjudged the students who had shown the greatest promise and both were invited back for the following term when Hogan would be installed as Holmes's second-in-charge with the hope that in due course he would take over the teaching with McMullen as his deputy.

Eugene Seitz declared the the ground-breaking classes an unqualified success as did the Commissioner of Police, Stafford Symonds in a long-winded speech which caused an outbreak of fidgeting amongst the audience and a stifled yawn or two. All the same, he was given a rousing round of applause when his speech came to an end…eventually!

Two days later we departed from New York for Fall River. Holmes had decided that we would take the Fall River Line, saying that he had been assured by Hogan that it was the only way to travel. This was a famed steamboat route; songs had been written about it apparently, which would take us through Long Island Sound, up to Narragansett Bay, arriving in Fall River early morning. The voyage was usually no more than eight hours.

Earlier we said our temporary farewells to Frank and Lavinia Kuhns and with our bags packed we hailed a cab to take us to the line's own Hudson River Dock in Manhattan. Embarkation was just a matter of moments and a steward showed us to our quarters on the *Priscilla*, a huge side-wheeled steamboat which was the last word in grandeur according to the steward. I ambled around the decks and peered into various state-rooms and I had to agree with the steward. Of its type it was possibly even grander than the *SS Bremen*. On returning to our quarters, Holmes had a question for me.

"If you don't feel the need for sleep just yet, Watson, would you mind if I went over some of the facts of the Borden case with you? Nothing concentrates my mind more than re-stating facts such as these to someone else and I know you will favour me with your pertinacious comments."

"I know a little of the case from the excellent library at the college, but I am perfectly willing to have you educate me further."

"Thank you."

Holmes cleared his throat and began:

"Shortly after eleven o'clock on the morning of Thursday, August 4th, 1892, a heavy, hot summer day from all accounts, at 92 Second Street in Fall River, Bridget Sullivan, the hired girl in the household of Andrew J. Borden, resting in her attic room, was startled to hear Lizzie Borden, Andrew's daughter, cry out, "Maggie, come down!"

"Who is Maggie?"

"Maggie was the name of an earlier maid employed by the Bordens; bizarrely they chose to call Bridget, Maggie. "What's the matter?" Bridget asked. "Come down quick! Father's dead! Somebody's come in and killed him!" Andrew Borden, seventy years old was one of the richest men in Fall River, a director on the boards of several banks, a commercial landlord whose holdings were considerable. He was a tall, thin, white-haired dour man, known for his thrift and admired for his business abilities. He chose to live with his second wife and his two grown spinster daughters in a small house in an unfashionable part of town, close to his business interests. He was not particularly likable, but, despite the frugal nature of their daily lives, moderately generous to his wife and daughters or so it appeared."

"When Bridget hurried downstairs, she found Lizzie standing at the back door. Lizzie stopped her from going into the sitting room, saying, "Don't go in there. Go and get the doctor. Run." Bridget ran across the street to their neighbour and family physician, Dr. Bowen. He was out, but Bridget told Mrs. Bowen that Mr. Borden had been killed. Bridget ran back to the house, and Lizzie sent her to summon the Borden sisters' friend, Miss Alice Russell, who lived a few blocks away. In the meanwhile, the neighbour to the north, Mrs. Adelaide Churchill, saw that something distressful was happening at the Borden house. She called across to Lizzie, who was at the back entrance to the house and asked if anything was wrong. Lizzie responded by saying, "Oh, Mrs. Churchill, please come over! Someone has killed Father!

Mrs. Churchill asked, "Where is your mother?" Lizzie said that she did not know and that Abby Borden, her stepmother, had received a note asking her to respond to someone who was sick. She told Mrs. Churchill that Bridget was unable to find Dr. Bowen. Mrs. Churchill volunteered to send her handyman to find a doctor and to send him to a telephone to summon help. The police station, about four hundred yards from 92 Second Street, received a message to respond to an incident at No. 92 at eleven-fifteen a.m."

"Is this the accepted version of events, Holmes?"

"It's certainly one of them for not only did the various witnesses often contradict those of other witnesses, they often contradicted themselves. This version, we could say, certainly initially, comes from Lizzie and the maid."

"Not an easy task then, to sift out the truth."

"Quite so. To continue, after sending her handy man and informing a passer-by of the trouble, Mrs. Churchill returned to the Borden kitchen. Dr. Bowen had arrived, along with Bridget, who had hurried back from informing Miss Russell. Dr. Bowen examined the body and asked for a sheet to cover it. Bridget said, "If I knew where Mrs. Whitehead, Abby Borden's younger sister, was, I would go and see if Mrs. Borden was there and tell her that Mr. Borden was very sick." Lizzie said, "Maggie, I am almost positive I heard her coming in. Go upstairs and see." Bridget refused, fearful of going upstairs alone, as she later explained. Mrs. Churchill volunteered to go up and see if Abby had returned. Bridget reluctantly went with her. The two went up the front staircase together and before they reached the landing they were able to see that Mrs. Borden was lying on the floor of the guestroom. Bridget saw Mrs. Borden's body. Mrs. Churchill rushed by her, viewed the obviously dead body and rushed downstairs, saying quite heartlessly in my view, "There's another one!""

"Abby Borden apparently provided, within the limits of Andrew's penuriousness, a comfortable home for her husband, who clearly appreciated her. Her stepdaughters were not particularly close to her. Lizzie, in fact, had been calling her, "Mrs. Borden" for the past several years, rather than, "Mother." In the meantime, Alice Russell had arrived, and Dr. Bowen, having left for a brief time to telegraph Lizzie's older sister Emma who was visiting friends in the neighbouring town of Fairhaven, had returned, and resumed examining Andrew Borden's body. It was on its right side on the sofa, feet still resting on the floor. His head was bent slightly to the right and his face had been cut by eleven blows. One eye had been cut in half and was protruding from his face, his nose had been severed. Most of the cuts were within a small area extending from the eye and nose to the ear. Blood was still seeping from the wounds. There were spots of blood on the floor, on the wall above the sofa and on a picture hanging on the wall. It appeared that he had been attacked from above and behind him as he slept."

"What a savage attack on a defenceless man, Holmes. It's a wicked world."

Holmes continued as if I hadn't spoken. "On climbing the stairs, the doctor found that Mrs. Borden had been struck more than a dozen times, from the back. The autopsy later revealed that there had been nineteen blows. Her head had been crushed by the same hatchet or axe that had presumably killed Mr. Borden, with one misdirected blow striking the back of her scalp, almost at the neck. The blood on Mrs. Borden's body was dark and congealed. Within minutes of receiving the call at eleven-fifteen, the City Marshal, Rufus B. Hilliard, dispatched Officer George W. Allen to the Borden house. He ran the four hundred yards to the house, saw that Andrew Borden was dead, and deputised a passer-by, Charles Sawyer, to stand guard while he went back to the stationhouse for assistance. Within minutes of his return, seven additional officers went to the murder scene. By eleven-forty five, the Medical Examiner, William Dolan, passing by the Borden house and noting the flurry of activity, was on the scene. Thus, the discovery of at least one murder happened at ten minutes after eleven, and within the next thirty-five minutes, the authorities were on the scene."

"The murder investigation, chaotic and stumbling as it was, can be reconstructed from the four official judicial events in the Lizzie Borden case: The inquest, the preliminary hearing, the Grand Jury hearing, and the trial. Basically, a circumstantial case against Lizzie was developed without the precise identification of a murder weapon, with no incriminating physical evidence for example, blood-stained clothes and no clear and convincing motive. Also, the case against Lizzie was hampered by the inability of the investigators to produce a corroborated demonstration of time and opportunity for the murders.

The investigation found that four events of significance occurred on August 3rd. The first was that Abby Borden had gone across the street to Dr. Bowen at seven in the morning, claiming that she and Andrew were being poisoned. Both of them had been violently ill during the night. Dr. Bowen told her that he did not think that her nausea and vomiting was serious, and sent her home. Later, he went across the street to check on Andrew, who ungraciously told him that he was not ill, and that he would not pay for an unsolicited house call. Bridget had also been ill that morning. However, no evidence of poisoning was found during the autopsies of Andrew and Abby."

"The second was that Lizzie had attempted to buy ten cents worth of prussic acid from Eli Bence, a clerk at Smith's Drug Store. She told Bence that she wanted the poison to kill insects in her sealskin cape. Bence refused to sell it to her without a prescription. Two others, a customer and another clerk, identified Lizzie as having been in the drugstore somewhere between ten and eleven-thirty in the morning. Lizzie denied that she had tried to buy prussic acid, testifying at the inquest that she had been out that morning, but not to Smith's Drug Store, then changing her story by saying that she had not left the house at all until the evening of the 3rd."

"Third, early in the afternoon, Uncle John Morse arrived. He was without luggage, but intended to stay overnight, so that he could visit relatives across town the next day. Both he and Lizzie testified that they did not see each other until after the murders the next day, although Lizzie knew that he was there. Finally, that evening Lizzie visited her friend, Miss Alice Russell. According to Miss Russell, Lizzie was agitated and worried over some threat, real or perceived to her father and concerned that something was about to happen. Miss Russell did her best to re-assure her and Lizzie returned home about nine o'clock, heard Uncle John and her parents talking loudly in the sitting room and went upstairs to bed without seeing them.

"The morning of the murder began with Bridget beginning her duties about six-fifteen. Uncle John was also up. Abby came down about seven, Andrew a few minutes later. They had breakfast. Lizzie remained upstairs until a few minutes after Uncle John left, at about eight-forty five. Andrew left for his business rounds around nine o'clock, according to Mrs. Churchill, the neighbour to the north. He visited the various banks where he was a stockholder and a store he owned that was being remodelled. He left for home around ten-forty, according to the carpenters working at the store. Just before nine o'clock, Abby instructed Bridget to wash the windows while she went upstairs to straighten up the guestroom where Uncle John had spent the night."

"Sometime between nine and ten Abby was killed in the guestroom. She had not gone out. The note that Lizzie said Abby had received from a sick friend, asking her to visit, was never found, despite an intensive search. Lizzie said that she might have inadvertently burned it. Andrew returned shortly after ten-forty. Bridget was washing the inside of the windows. Because the door was locked from the inside with three locks, Bridget had to let Mr. Borden in. As she fumbled with the lock, she testified that she heard Lizzie laugh from the upstairs landing. However, Lizzie told the police that she had been in the kitchen when her father came home."

"Mr. Borden, who had kept his and Mrs. Borden's bedroom locked since a burglary the year before, took the key to his bedroom off the mantle and went up the back stairs. Lizzie set up the ironing board and began to iron handkerchiefs. For a few minutes more, Bridget resumed washing windows."

"Bridget went up to her room to lie down about five minutes before eleven. Andrew went to the couch in the sitting room for a nap. Lizzie went out into the yard, or to the barn, or to the barn loft, no one seems quite sure, least of all Lizzie, for twenty to thirty minutes. Where she had precisely gone was she was vague about. She said that her purpose for going to the barn was to find some metal for fishing sinkers, since she intended to join Emma at Fairhaven, although Emma knew nothing of that intention, to do some fishing. When she returned at ten minutes past eleven, she found her father dead."

"Over the course of several weeks, investigators were able to construct a time-table of events covering the period of Wednesday, August 3rd, the day before the murders, through to Sunday, August seventh, the day that Miss Russell saw Lizzie burning a dress, an act that proved crucial at the inquest. The police investigation now began in earnest. Officer Mullaly asked Lizzie if there were any hatchets in the house. "Yes, she said. "They are everywhere." She then told Bridget to show him where they were. Mullaly and Bridget went down to the basement and found four hatchets, one with dried blood and hair on it; cow's blood and hair, as it was later determined, a second rusty claw-headed hatchet, and two that were dusty. One of these was without a handle and covered in ashes. The break appeared to be recent. This was the hatchet that was submitted in evidence. About this time, Uncle John returned, strolling into the backyard, picking some pears and eating them. He had been asked by Andrew that morning to return for the noon meal. He later testified that he did not notice if the cellar door was open or closed."

"Sergeant Harrington and another officer, having questioned Lizzie as to her whereabouts during the morning, examined the barn loft where Lizzie said she had been looking for metal for fishing sinkers. They found that the loft floor was thick with dust, with no evidence that anyone had been up there. At three o'clock, the bodies of Andrew and Abby were carried into the dining room, where Dr. Dolan performed autopsies on them as they lay on the dining room table. Their stomachs were removed and tied, and sent by special messenger to Dr. Wood at Harvard."

"Meanwhile, upstairs, Deputy Marshal John Fleet questioned Lizzie, asking her if she had any idea of who could have committed the murders. Other than a man with whom her father had had an argument a few weeks before, a man unknown to her, she knew of no one. When asked directly if Uncle John Morse or Bridget could have killed her father and mother, she said that they couldn't have. Uncle John had left the house at eight-forty five and Bridget was upstairs when Mr. Borden was killed. She pointedly reminded Mr. Fleet that Abby was not her mother, but her stepmother."

"Emma returned from Fairhaven just before seven that evening. The bodies of the Bordens were still on the dining room table, awaiting the arrival of the undertaker. Sergeant Harrington continued the questioning of Lizzie. Finally, the police left, leaving a cordon around the house to keep away the large number of curious Fall River citizens who had been gathered around the front of the house since noon. Bridget was taken to stay with a neighbour, Alice Russell stayed in the Bordens' bedroom, Emma and Lizzie in their respective bedrooms and Uncle John, rather surprisingly in the guest room where Abby had met her violent end."

"He must be made of stern stuff this John Morse. I am not sure I would welcome sleeping in a room where a vicious murder had been committed hours earlier."

"Indeed, Watson."

"You have obviously delved into this case very deeply."

"Something about it has held a fascination for me these past five years, a case which seemed so simple at the outset yet became more complicated with each piece of so-called evidence and each fresh witness statement."

"Lizzie was acquitted because of a lack of evidence? I suppose what I mean is, do the people of Fall River believe her to be guilty, but absolved of the crime due to there being no clear-cut evidence of her guilt?"

"Apparently, Watson, they do."

"And what is your feeling on the matter, Holmes?"

"I will reserve final judgment until the end of our stay in Fall River. I, of course, will be most interested to hear your verdict so I will not try to bias your findings with any half-formed conclusions of my own at this stage."

"If there was such a lack of evidence, how did it ever come to trial?"

"It may not have had it not been for the dress."

"The dress?"

"To explain, Watson, On Sunday morning, Miss Russell observed Lizzie burning a dress in the kitchen stove. She said, "If I were you, I wouldn't let anybody see me do that, Lizzie." Lizzie said it was a dress stained with paint, and was of no use. It was this testimony at the inquest that prompted Judge Blaisdell of the Second District Court to charge Lizzie with the murders. She was held in Taunton Jail, which had facilities for female prisoners. The preliminary hearing which followed on from the inquest was also held before Judge Blaisdell. He declared that Lizzie was probably guilty of the murders and bound her over to appear before the Grand Jury which had the result of Lizzie being sent for trial which was set for June the following year."

I let an involuntary yawn at that stage which Holmes seized on as a sign of boredom! I assured him that was not the case, but I felt in urgent need of sleep. I assured him further that I would look forward with interest to the the next instalment in the morning, by which time we would be in Fall River.

"Very well, Watson, you sleep and I will apprise your further tomorrow when we spend the day at leisure looking into all things Borden."

I was asleep in no time at all, but before I slid into the arms of Morpheus, I imagined a day of inactivity save for maybe poring over court records and witness statements. Once again, events overtook us and our first day in Fall River was very different than either one of us could have imagined.

Lizzie Borden

Chapter Eight

We breakfasted early on the *Priscilla* and only briefly touched on the subject of the Lizzie Borden affair. Hogan had promised to meet us and we spotted his tall figure amongst a smattering of people on the quayside as we disembarked.

He had a strained look on his face and was lost in thought even as he greeted us.

"Mr Homes, Dr Watson, I am so pleased that you have arrived. There has been a murder!" he blurted out.

"Is murder a rarity in Fall River?" asked Holmes.

"Homicide is not exactly common here, but this particular murder is a little out of the ordinary. I'll explain in the cab; if you don't mind, we will meet my uncle at the scene, he is desirous of your help."

We clambered into the cab and waited while young Hogan collected his thoughts once more.

"Around two hours ago…"

"Around? Come now, Hogan, you know better than that, please be exact in every detail."

"Very well then. At six forty this morning the body of Sansom Weinberger was discovered at the drugstore he owned on Locust Street. His assistant James Duggan could not gain entry from the front of the store so went to the rear of the store. The back door was wide open. He called his employer's name and getting no response climbed the stairs to Weinberger's apartment. There he found his employer covered in blood. Mr Holmes, he had been hit with an axe anything up to twenty times. No money or effects have been stolen as far as my uncle's men have ascertained. This was an act of murderous rage."

"Go on, Hogan, there is more I suspect."

"Sansom Weinberger is one of two chemists in the city who refused to sell Lizzie Borden prussic acid just prior to the murders."

"A coincidence surely. You are not suggesting that Lizzie Borden killed Weinberger?"

"Word has travelled fast and my uncle has had the foresight to post a guard outside 'Maplecroft' the house where Lizzie and Emma now live. I fear if we cannot find the culprit soon then things may turn very ugly indeed."

"From the accounts I have read, Miss Borden only attempted to buy prussic acid from one drugstore, Eli Bence at…"

"Smiths Drugstore, Holmes. I did give the case rather more than a cursory look while in the college library and I was awake enough to follow your account of yesterday evening."

"Thank you, Watson, so it would seem. Hogan?"

"The visit you mention was detailed to the Grand Jury prior to indictment, but was ruled inadmissible at the trial meaning there was no point in trying to procure or bring forth extra evidence of this kind."

"Thank you, Hogan. I find it hard that anyone would credit Lizzie Borden with being the perpetrator. What would they be suggesting; that she waited five years for some form of revenge knowing that she would be the chief suspect? It all seems very tenuous. It's more likely that someone used this method of murder to try and implicate her. The fact that she knew and had dealings with Weinberger was perhaps a lucky circumstance for our killer. Still, we have no data yet and we must guard against forming too many fanciful theories."

"I would guess that not too many of your theories are fanciful, Mr Holmes."

"Some may appear so at the outset," I said, "but the end result is usually a loss of liberty for someone."

Before we could reach Hogan's uncle another police vehicle drew alongside us. An officer leaned out and shouted across to Hogan.

"Change of plan, young Mike. Follow me to North Main Street."

Our driver spurred the horses on and we clattered through the city at a gallop, keeping the other vehicle in our sight. The drivers were like madmen like their cabby counterparts of New York; I was expecting one or other of the two vehicles to topple over given the way they handled each junction and corner. I was extremely relieved to see the sign that marked the beginning of North Main Street. There was abundant activity outside one of the buildings, police officers milling around, an ambulance drawn up outside, the usual onlookers who are drawn to scenes of crime and this surely was such a scene.

A short, but burly man struggled through the crowd and came towards us. He had the countenance of one who has suddenly found himself out of his depth. He stretched out a hand to us.

"You must be Sherlock Holmes and Dr Watson, pleased to meet you. I am Elmer Hogan, Mike's uncle."

"A pleasure, Chief Hogan," Holmes rejoined. "Homicide?"

"A particularly nasty one. A woman by the name of Honoria Walters. Her husband returned after completing his night's work at Metacomet Mill to find his wife's mutilated body in the kitchen. She had been struck numerous times with what the doctor thinks must be an axe or hatchet. In view of that I have asked the officers who are currently posted outside Lizzie Borden's house to bring her in."

"Is there a connection between the two women?" asked Holmes.

"Honoria Walters managed a local clothing store, specialising in the latest east coast fashions. A few weeks ago Mrs Walters caught Lizzie attempting to steal a few items and threatened to go to the police."

"Did she carry out this threat?"

"No, Mr Holmes."

"Then how come you to know of it?"

"Whispers, Mr Holmes, whispers. The exchange was overheard by certain members of Fall River society who seemed to think it was beholden on them to broadcast the matter to all and sundry in their circles. There is some history regarding this for Andrew Borden, Lizzie's father, had to placate various shopkeepers and recompense them for goods Lizzie had stolen, although let me say that I have no proof that Lizzie ever stole anything, but as you know, there is no smoke without fire. Do you want to view the body in situ?"

"If we may, yes."

I had never become entirely hardened to the sight of a victim of a violent death despite the number of times I had encountered them. Those that can inflict violence on another in pursuit of often petty reasons, I have never understood. Particularly, when such crimes are premeditated and carried out with such ferocity as I was no doubt about to witness. I braced myself as we walked into the apartment.

The Walters' apartment occupied the lower part of the building, comprising two floors of this six storey building. The rear door led into a hallway, the second door of that hallway took us into the kitchen where Honoria Walters lay in a pool of blood. The viciousness of the attack was apparent by the splashes of blood which adorned the surfaces and wall. Merciful indeed it would have been if the first blow had succeeded in killing her, but the blood told a different tale.

"Is there any sign of a break-in?" Holmes asked the senior Hogan.

"None whatsoever. The door could have been unlocked anyway. I have not had the opportunity to question the husband, Charlie for he is so distraught I am giving him a little time to compose himself."

"You are aware of course…"

"Yes, Mr Holmes, the husband is always the chief suspect and rightly so only too often," Hogan replied with just a touch of impatience in his voice.

We both studied the wreck of a human being on the kitchen floor, vibrant and alive one moment and life snuffed out the very next. She had sustained at least six separate blows to the head, obviously meted out with great force. She was still alive after, at least the first blow for there were tell-tales signs of defensive wounds on her arms where she had desperately strived to ward of her attacker's blows.

"The police doctor has already attended?"

"Yes, Mr Holmes. He has estimated the time of death as around one in the morning with a leeway of thirty minutes either side of that time."

"Watson?"

I gave the body a cursory check and informed Holmes that I would tend to agree with the police doctor's estimate but that this may be due for some revision later when the autopsy would be carried out.

Holmes nodded. "Shall we see if Mr Walters has recovered his composure sufficiently enough to speak with us?"

Hogan showed to a small parlour where Mr Walters was sitting in a high-backed chair, looking absolutely wracked with grief. Incongruously, two uniformed officers flanked him as if expecting their charge to bolt for the door at any moment. I looked across at Holmes pointedly and tried to make my message clear, 'be gentle with this man.'

Holmes drew up a chair and seated himself opposite Walters. "My name is Sherlock Holmes; I am a visitor to this city and indeed these shores. I have a certain reputation as regards solving crime and you can rest assured I will be leaving no stone unturned in finding the perpetrator of this heinous act. Now, I know this is hard for you, but questions have to be asked and answered. When you arrived home from the mill this morning, did everything appear normal as far as you could tell?"

"Up until the moment I entered the house yes…"

"Was the door unlocked?"

"Yes…um…I think so."

"Was it the normal practice of your wife to lock the door while you were working the night shift?"

"Yes, I guess it was, but she was always up before I arrived home and had the door unlocked."

"But, either way, you had a key?"

"Yes, I always carry one."

"The police doctor has offered his expert opinion that your wife was sadly murdered around one o' clock this morning. Assuming the door was locked when she retired for the evening, could you think of anyone that she might unlock the door to or any circumstances in which that may be a possibility?"

"No, I can think of no one. We rarely see the neighbours; in fact the family in the apartment next door are away at present. We have no family in the city."

"What time did you start work, Mr Walters?"

"The night shift starts at nine and I leave the apartment around eight-thirty."

"Is there a clocking in procedure followed at the mill?" asked Chief Hogan.

"Hey, what is this? Checking up on me? I was at the mill all night and yes we clock in and clock out. My wife is lying dead there and you have the gall to suspect me. What I suggest, is that you go out and look for this crazed madman and leave me alone."

Holmes said, "Chief Hogan is only doing his job. The process of elimination is an important part of the primary investigation and will certainly be of the utmost assistance in apprehending your wife's killer. Just one or two more questions if I may."

"Go ahead if you must."

"What time did you leave the mill?"

"Slightly earlier than usual, around seven-thirty, it had quietened down by then. I oversee a small team in the dispatch department and the comings and goings of carts and wagons had lessened by then."

"Do you work straight through the shift? If it's as busy as you say, then it can be no easy thing to take a break."

"Our employer insists that we have a break. He reckons it maximises our potential and output. I had mine at two-thirty, in the company of two of my team if you must know."

"Thank you, Mr Walters, you have been most helpful. I am sorry for your loss."

A commotion in the kitchen signalled the arrival of the mortuary team who would load the body onto their vehicle and remove Honoria Walters to where she would face her necessary final indignity. We had to restrain Charles Walters who dashed from his chair and made for the door. I eased the man back in his seat. My eyes alighted on a small bottle of brandy and I poured some into a small tumbler and urged him to drink. After he had calmed down, we excused ourselves for we had the unpleasant, but necessary duty to fulfil of attending another scene of bloody death.

The short ride to Locust Street took place in complete silence. At the outset, Chief Hogan had asked Holmes for his impression of Charlie Walters, but had not been favoured with a response which had the effect of setting the tone for the journey. There were no crowds to be seen at the drug store that Weinberger had owned for the excitement, as far as the onlookers concerned, was long over. One of the officers posted outside confirmed to his chief that the body of Sansom Weinberger had been carried off to the mortuary, a fact that caused an audible sound of exasperation from Holmes.

"I suppose we can always visit the mortuary later eh, Watson?"

"Certainly, Holmes."

"Excellent. Chief, your nephew tells me that a James Duggan discovered the body of his employer just after six-forty this morning and that the body was upstairs?"

"Correct, Mr Holmes."

A solitary policeman at the rear of the premises stood smartly to attention and swung open the door for us. Directly ahead of us was a carpeted set of stairs which creaked as we ascended them.

"The door was open when Duggan arrived yes?"

"Wide open he said," replied the Chief.

When we entered the sitting-room of the apartment, it struck me how little blood there was compared with the scene we had just witnessed on North Main Street. Evidently, Weinberger had been fortunate, if I can term it such, to be dispatched by the first blow. The killer had not just been content to end the man's life for his murderous rage continued on in spite of the certain knowledge that Weinberger had long since departed this world.

"I noticed the passageway by the side of the stairs; would I be correct in thinking that it gives direct access to the rear of the store?"

"Quite so, Mr Holmes," averred Michael Hogan.

"So we can construct a scenario where Weinberger was, assuming he was asleep, wakened by a knocking at the door."

"If indeed the door was locked, Holmes. We have no evidence to suggest it was."

"We have the evidence of our own eyes, Watson, for surely no man would go to his slumber allowing all and sundry a route into his store."

Holmes walked down the stairs to the door with us in his wake and examined the bolts, drew them back and forth a few times and sniffed the mechanism.

"Recently oiled," he remarked, "in our construction of events then, Weinberger hears a knocking on the door and comes down the stairs. He shouts through the door to ascertain who is outside."

"Unless it was a pre-arranged meeting, Holmes."

"There is that possibility, Watson although it is I fear a remote one. Once he is satisfied, he draws back the bolts, turns the key and admits his visitor. Now, if that visitor was Lizzie Borden, then there are problems facing us. Given Lizzie's past, would he be likely to admit her? Perhaps he was one of those who believed her guilty of the crimes with which she was charged, so once again, why would he admit her?

"Perhaps there was, shall we say, an understanding between them, in which case, she would be freely admitted," suggested young Hogan.

"If there was, surely in a small city as this, someone would have got wind of it. Miss Borden is after all, one of the city's more infamous residents."

"But it's not impossible that for reasons of his own that he did admit her," I ventured.

"If we assume he did and she was in the grip of a murderous rage then why did she not strike him down at once? We can apply that to the scene we just witnessed too. The circumstances do not sit comfortably with this view of Lizzie Borden as an avenging angel, making her way through the dark streets with an axe, waiting for her moments of revenge. It seems contrived, as though it's something we are meant to be seeing."

"Surely, Holmes at this early stage there is not sufficient data to come to that conclusion."

"Thank you, Watson for keeping me flat-footed on the ground. You are right of course."

Holmes raced back up to the stairs to the sitting-room and began a minute search of the room. Within a few moments after much shaking of his head, he disappeared into what turned out to be the bedroom. Lying stretched out on the bed he brought the pillows to his nose and inhaled deeply. Nodding, as if he had decided on a course of action, he followed an invisible trail around the apartment like a bloodhound on the trail of aniseed.

"What was it that you found so interesting on the pillow," I asked.

"Perfume, Watson. I am not familiar with it although it shares certain characteristics of 'The Seine by Moonlight' a favoured French perfume."

"A lady was present then."

"Well deduced, Watson! The identity of the woman will have to remain a mystery for now; the apartment has yielded no further clues as to her identity. A visit to Fall River's finest perfumery however may be of the greatest benefit. Did the doctor who attended give a time of death?"

"In broad terms, Mr Holmes, death was very close to the time given for Mrs Walters," replied the Chief.

"And Weinberger was clad in his nightshirt only?"

"Quite so."

"Excellent," said Holmes, rubbing his hands together. "I think I have seen all I need to see, gentlemen. Is it possible that we can be deposited at our lodgings? I am sure we both need to freshen up before taking our next steps."

"Certainly, Mr Holmes, I will organise that for you now. Do you wish to come down to headquarters and interview Miss Borden?"

"Not at this juncture no, my first port of call will be to a perfumery, perhaps you can point me in the right direction."

"Carr's on West Street will be your man. Lionel Carr supplies the city with the finest perfumes and colognes, my wife can verify that for you as can my wallet." replied the Chief.

"My thanks to your wife in that case. By the way, is there a known connection between Sansom Weinberger and Honoria Walters save for the tenuous link of both having had dealings with Lizzie Borden?" asked Holmes.

"I am not aware of one, but if there should be one, I am sure we can uncover it," replied the senior Hogan.

His nephew spoke up. "There is a possibility they may have met at the regular Chamber of Commerce meetings. Although Mrs Walters did not own the clothing store, she pretty much ran it single-handed and may well have attended such meetings if only to show the men-folk of the town that women have brains attuned to business too."

"Excellent reasoning, I'm sure that information can be ascertained without too much hardship."

"I will undertake to find the information we require, that is if my uncle is agreeable."

"Please do, it will release a little more man power for me and I am not your chief anymore, but, Mike, just do as I say anyway!"

The Chief went outside and spoke to one of the officers still in attendance.

"We will utilise the vehicle we have out there to transport you to Second Street, the driver will then return for us."

"Thank you. Next door to the Borden murder house eh, Watson?"

"And, Mr Holmes, with access to it too. Mr O' Hara who currently rents the house from the Borden sisters is perfectly willing to open his doors to you as I have promised him you will be courteous and respectful at all times unlike some he has admitted who try to take away certain fixtures and fittings as souvenirs. He would appreciate it if you try and time your visits, if more than one be needed, to what he terms sensible times of day."

"We will endeavour to comply with Mr O' Hara's requests at all times and all things being well, we will liaise with you later at police headquarters. Goodbye."

The ride was again a short one and in no time at all we found ourselves on Borden Street which led us into Second Street and there we had our first sight of the scene of the infamous Borden murders.

North Main Street, Fall River

The Borden house

Andrew Borden

Chapter Nine

I wasn't sure what I was expecting; the sinister house that existed in my head had a Gothic, eerie look to it, whilst the reality was a fairly ordinary looking timber-clad house. It was, I suppose, a striking building only in comparison with the cape-styled building next door which was to be our base. Built over three floors, it occupied a reasonably large plot with a well-manicured lawn and tidy outbuildings. Fancifully, in spite of its ordinariness, I felt it exuded evil in some undefinable way.

Number 94 was our initial destination and waiting on the doorstep to greet us was a giant of a man with the biggest beard I had ever seen. It was debatable whether its downward growth or outward growth was the greater. He introduced himself to us as Peter Jubb and took our bags from us as though he were picking up feathers. He carried them, one swinging from each giant hand as he ascended the stairs.

"These are the only two rooms I have, gentlemen. I think you will find them comfortable enough," he announced as he pointed out a suite of rooms on the second floor."

"Thank you. Mr Jubb, tell me, were you residing here at the time of the murders?" I asked.

"Well, you know, if I had a dollar for every time I have been asked this question, I would be a wealthy man. No, I have been living here for just these past three years, nor did I know the family, save from what everyone knows of the Bordens, They are perhaps the most prominent family in Fall River. My brother, William, is quite familiar with Lizzie and until quite recently has been on very good terms with her."

"I have the impression that she has very few friends in the city, your brother must be a true friend and non-judgmental."

"He is a minister, involved with the Central Congregational Church here. Lizzie took refuge in religion, especially in the few weeks after the murders. She was also active or seen to be active, or perhaps you could say, wanted to be seen in the Christian Endeavor Society and the Woman's Christian Temperance Union."

"You seem to doubt her faith, Mr Jubb?"

"I have no real reason to do so and my brother believes her faith to be genuine and that she turned to God because she needed succour at that time. Some may see it as a cynical attempt to curry favour. I guess I fall into the latter camp."

"Miss Borden certainly stirs up the emotions in the city and most of the views I have heard coincide with your view. I am given to wondering whether anyone believes in her innocence in Fall River," Holmes stated.

"You would be hard pushed to find anyone save for her sister, Emma and I am none too sure of her even."

"I still find it extraordinary," I said, "that she can be acquitted of all charges, exonerated and walk free from court only to be met with all this ongoing hostility."

"If you lived here, you may feel differently."

Mr Jubb left us to unpack, which we accomplished fairly quickly. Although I was more than a little fatigued after the events of the morning, I agreed to accompany Holmes to Carr's perfumery. West Street was only a short distance from Second Street and the perfumery was easily located by following one's nose. The scents in the shop I found heady and almost overpowering. It was a riot of floral aromas mixed with eastern spices which told their own tales.

The florid looking gentleman behind the well-stocked counter greeted us with a cheery hello and asked us how he could help.

"I am looking for a perfume which has a familial scent not unlike 'The Seine by Moonlight'. I feel sure that you will know exactly what I mean."

"Ah yes, how nice to meet a discerning customer, the scent you are looking for is 'Midnight in Paris'." He reached his hand up to the shelf behind him and selected an exquisite looking bottle. "Here we are, sir. I think, if I may say so, that madam will be impressed."

"If I may?" said Holmes and took the bottle from him. He brought it to his nose, sniffed and nodded. "That is the very one I am looking for."

"Shall I wrap the bottle, sir? Maybe sir would like a card attached expressing your sentiments?"

"That will not be necessary; I merely wanted to inhale the scent. Good day to you, sir."

"Well, of all the…thank you for your *custom*, sir."

"Perhaps you could help me further by telling me if you have any customers known to you who use this perfume regularly?"

"I think not. Good day, *sir*."

Even Holmes could see that no amount of persuasion on his part would have the result of Mr Carr enlightening us.

"Is that knowledge of any practical use to us, Holmes?" I asked as we exited the perfumery.

"Anything we can discover, no matter how trivial it may seem, can have some bearing on the case."

"I am sure that is so, but let's not forget our real reason for being here which is to help Emma Borden find the truth about her father and stepmother's deaths."

"The two incidents are connected in some way, if only in the minds of others and we can scarcely ignore one at the expense of the other. We could do as Chief Hogan suggested and stroll across to the Central Police Station and have an audience with Lizzie herself. What do you say, Watson?"

"It would be of the utmost interest to me to meet the woman."

"Excellent. Best foot forward then."

After spending a frustrating few minutes in attempting to explain to an officious desk sergeant just who we were and why we needed to see Chief Elmer Hogan, we were eventually shown to his office. He presented a mournful countenance to us and the excitement of the day had obviously caught up with him.

"Hello, gentlemen, did you find what you wanted from Lionel Carr?"

"The perfume I could smell on Weinberger's pillows was one with the exotic name of 'Midnight in Paris'. It is I am sure you will agree a starting point in our investigation."

"It seems to be a clear case of search for the woman then and ascertain what part she has to play in this affair beyond the obvious."

"I presume your men are searching 'Maplecroft'?"

"Yes, there has been no report of anything untoward so far although, how's this, I will send a message to the house and ask that a search may be made for this perfume you name, Mr Holmes. If we find it, it may be a clincher and perhaps Weinberger's lady friend was Lizzie Borden herself. Perhaps they had words, a lover's tiff and things went too far."

"I see…and then Lizzie grabs the axe which is conveniently to hand and puts her side of the argument forcefully. I am not familiar with Fall River idiosyncrasies and etiquette, but I would imagine keeping an axe in the bedroom does not figure too prominently amongst them."

"She could have gone downstairs to cool off and then returned with an axe," the Chief said.

"Weinberger lives in an apartment, what need would he have for an axe or hatchet?"

"I do see that there are arguments against such a theory, but all the same, I will send that message to my men at 'Maplecroft'."

After he had done so he invited us to the holding cells to see Lizzie. Holmes insisted that if we were to interview her then he would rather it take place in different, more congenial surroundings. Hogan agreed that it was probably a good idea and invited us into an empty office on the second floor, empty save for a desk and two chairs.

A short while later Hogan entered the room with Lizzie Borden who cut an abject figure, manacled as she was to an officer. Abject, yes, but strangely proud, almost dignified, at least that's how I saw her. She was small of stature, but she seemed to dominate the room somehow, her presence was powerful indeed. Holmes asked if the manacles could be removed. The officer looked at Hogan who nodded his silent assent. I invited Lizzie to sit, which she did hesitantly. I sat in the other chair and Holmes perched on the corner of the desk.

"Miss Borden, my name is Sherlock Holmes and this is my colleague Dr Watson. The other gentlemen you know of course, but they are just leaving."

"This is pretty irregular, Mr Holmes, I have to say, this is my case after all."

"Yes, Chief, and it will remain your case I assure you, but if you could indulge me just this once, I would be forever in your debt."

"Very well, Mr Holmes. I will leave you to it, Come on, Smith."

"Now, Miss Borden, can I fetch you anything? A drink maybe?"

Lizzie did not speak, but shook her head.

"Very well, now, do you know why you have been brought here?"

"Yes." The voice was clear and free of emotion.

"What is your connection to Sansom Weinberger?"

"I have none. I do not know the man."

"Some five years ago you attempted to purchase prussic acid from his drugstore."

Lizzie did not respond.

"Do you deny that was the case?"

"I may have done. I can't remember all my dealings from that time. If I did, what of it?"

"The police are suggesting that his murder may be an act of revenge by one who felt they had been wronged."

"I have nothing to say on the matter."

"This is a murder investigation; you would be well advised to keep nothing back."

"I do not know the man. I am sad that he has been murdered, I deplore the act, but I cannot help you further."

"You do not recall attempting to purchase poison from the man?"

"No," she answered with an emphatic shake of the head.

"Very well, perhaps you are more familiar with the name, Mrs Honoria Walters?"

"I do not recall the name."

"Miss Borden, just a few weeks ago I am given to understand that Mrs Walters caught you in the act of stealing items from the clothing store she manages, perhaps you cannot recall that event either."

"It was a misunderstanding. I am prone to forgetfulness and once I realised the situation I apologised and Mrs Walters, if it was her, accepted my apology."

"My understanding of the matter is that Mrs Walters threatened you with police action. This was in fact overheard by others in the store."

"Then I fear you understand very little. The truth is as I have told it. Why you choose to bring this matter up I do not know."

"The answer to that is simple; Mrs Walters too, has been murdered."

Lizzie's face remained blank, her features unmoved, registering neither shock or surprise at Holmes's words. Unblinking, she stared at Holmes.

"I am mighty sorry for the poor woman, but I cannot help you, you must search for your murderer elsewhere."

"Elmer Hogan will be asking you to account for your movements during the night, perhaps you can enlighten us?"

"I do not see I have the need to do so, but as you obviously feel that you can trample all over my privacy, I can tell you that I was at home all evening, but when I retired I found I could not sleep so I rose and left the house and just walked to clear my head. It's something I often do, for those pious and good folk of Fall River deny me the freedom to do as I like and go where I like without fingers being pointed in my direction. And yes, I hear the comments, the accusations and the spite in their voices. Is it any wonder I have taken to parading the streets under cover of darkness?"

"Was you sister aware that you had left the house?"

"I very much doubt it; she is in Concord visiting friends of the family. If only I had known I would need an alibi I would have asked her to cancel her visit," she responded with a sweet smile, but devilment in her eyes.

"Your sister, Emma has requested my help in ascertaining the truth of what befell your father and mother. Were you aware of that fact?"

"She was NOT my mother, she was my step-mother" she spat out. Emma is always wanting to know the truth of what happened that day, she can be rather tiresome on the subject."

"Do you not want to know the truth, Miss Borden or do you know it already?" asked Holmes pointedly.

"The dead are dead and buried, leave them be. They cannot be brought back to life even if anybody wished it."

"Would you wish it?"

"I have nothing further to say on the matter."

"Very well, although I certainly have a mind to tax your memory of that day at a future date. Do you use perfume, Miss Borden?"

"Your questions are most amusing, Mr Holmes. Why in the world would you ask such a thing?"

"It may have a bearing on these current crimes."

"As I know nothing of these crimes then I fail to see the relevance of your question, but as the answer is of supreme unimportance then I am willing to give you that answer. No I do not use perfume or any kind of scent."

"You are not aware of a perfume which rejoices in the name of 'Midnight in Paris'?"

"I have never heard of it. Will that be all? For, as you say, Elmer Hogan will want his turn now."

"Thank you for your help, Miss Borden, that will be all for now."

Holmes rapped on the door and Lizzie was escorted back to her cell.

"Well?" inquired the Chief. "What do you think, Mr Holmes?"

"She is, I believe, a very strong-willed woman, but if you want to know whether I believe her guilty or not, then you may have to be patient."

"Thank you Mr Holmes, the evidence points to her guilt and that is enough for me to go ahead and charge her."

"Chief Hogan," I protested, "you have no evidence to speak of unless it's a crime for Lizzie to have known these two people."

"Not only knew them, Dr Watson, but had run-ins with them. There were bad feelings and look at how the murders were committed, with an axe or hatchet."

"My dear Hogan," interrupted Holmes, "on that basis we must attribute every such murder in the whole of the United States to Lizzie

Borden! No, it will not do. Watson does have a point; there is no evidence as such."

"As to that, this is my case and you must allow me to run it as I see fit and I will apprise Marshal Hilliard of my suspicions and intent."

Mike Hogan entered the room at that point as the situation threatened to become heated.

"I have examined the attendance records for the Chamber of Commerce meetings and have spoken to one or two attendees. Sansom Weinberger and Honoria Walters both attended Chamber meetings over the last year. That is to say they were both in attendance at the same time. No one I spoke to could confirm whether they actually knew each other so to speak other than for exchanging pleasantries. The last few meetings, however, have been attended by one or other, never both of them."

"Excellent, young Hogan. Now we have another connection, however tenuous it may be."

"Does that fact take us any further forward?" I asked.

"Not necessarily, Watson, but it's something that can be docketed away and may yet prove to be useful to us. It's been a long day for us, gentlemen and I am sure Watson will be relieved if we bring it to a close; I propose that we retrace our steps to Second Street and ensconce ourselves in the luxury of Mr Jubb's guest house. Will you keep us informed as to further developments, gentlemen?"

"Gladly," answered the younger of the Hogan's. His uncle merely nodded and grunted.

"Well," asked Holmes as we walked towards Second Street, "what did you think of the infamous Miss Lizzie Borden? Your impressions may be invaluable to me as is often the case."

"She brought to my mind the image of a cobra, poised and ready to strike. I believe her to be a formidable woman who is capable of anything."

"Upon my word, Watson, she certainly made an impression on you and you her great defender too."

"I am none too sure I should be cast in the role of defender, Holmes, I have merely noted the incongruity of someone acquitted of all charges in a court of law, but declared guilty by so many people. Can anyone really know the truth of what happened that day?"

"That remains to be seen, but who knows, two old sleuth-hounds like us may yet find a scent which has remained dormant these last five years."

As we walked past the Borden house, I shivered involuntarily, but I was sure I was not alone in that. For everyone for whom the house held a morbid fascination there were no doubt others who gave it a wide berth.

Holmes's voice interrupted my reverie. "We could impinge on Mr O' Hara's hospitality and allow ourselves a glimpse of the house, Watson."

"By all means, if Mr O' Hara is agreeable."

Mr O' Hara proved to be entirely agreeable although not without the resigned look of one who has had to perform this role many times.

"I should charge a fee, gentlemen, that's what I should do. There is a fortune to be made out of misery and men's prurience I believe."

The house, to my mind, appeared ill-conceived as if just thrown together and left to fend for itself. The rooms were of disparate sizes and dimensions and had no clear identity.

"Have you made any changes?" I asked.

"No, sir, as a tenant, I am unable to do so. The house is virtually in its original state save for some alterations that Andrew Borden deemed necessary. I've grown used to the house and am, I profess, rather fond of it. There are many folk in town who would never sleep under its roof, you know, the kind who believe in spirits and suchlike. I can tell you, gentlemen, my sleep has never been disturbed."

He led us into a small parlour off the hallway. "Here is where Andrew Borden met his untimely end," he announced dramatically with a flourish and a wave of his arm towards a sofa up against the wall nearest the door."

"The very sofa he was murdered on?" I asked.

"The very same; Lizzie insisted a new cover was stitched on to it and that it remain in use. Quite a souvenir, don't you think?"

I found it perplexing that a piece of furniture so ill-used would remain in daily use, even allowing for the fact that Lizzie Borden no longer resided here and hence would not have to look at it. It struck me as cold-hearted in the extreme, had it been my father murdered so brutally I would have taken an axe to it and burned the remains.

"Shall we go upstairs?"

We followed O' Hara to the upper floor where he showed us the room, which was used as a guest room five years ago. The room was devoid of furniture apart from a bed.

"Abby Borden was found slumped by the side of the bed, this bed in fact. The uncle who was visiting had used this room and it's reckoned that Abby had come in to remove the sheets, although you would think that would be the maid's job, anyway she was struck down from behind. Dead before she hit the ground they say."

I tried to imagine the scene, the absolute horror of it and tried to understand the mind of a murderer who would even contemplate such an action against a defenceless woman and then to wait in determined silence for Andrew Borden to arrive home and strike him down in a similar brutal fashion.

Holmes had been strangely silent throughout our visit which only came to an end after examining every room in the house including the spacious cellar, as dark and dank place as I had ever known.

Mr Jubb had prepared a meal for us and as we partook, Holmes looked across at me intently, almost with a look of pain on his features and muttered, "Someone should pay for that evil, someone should pay."

Mike Hogan

Chapter Ten

We broke our fast quite late in the morning with both of us wondering what the day would bring, Holmes being particularly restless. As it turned out, we did not have long to wait for young Hogan appeared shortly after eleven o'clock to apprise us regarding the case.

"The search at 'Maplecroft' has been concluded, nothing was found that proved any connection between Lizzie and Weinberger and Mrs Walters, beyond the connection we are already aware of. A search was made for the perfume you mentioned, Mr Holmes, but none was found by that name although there were other scent bottles in the bathroom."

"So she lied then," I exclaimed.

"You forget, Watson, she is not the only woman in the house."

"Of course, I was forgetting Emma."

"I understand," continued Hogan, "that certain ladies, friends of Lizzie, occasionally sleep at the house too."

"I thought Fall River society shunned Lizzie. I am glad to see that is not entirely the case."

"As to that, Doctor, this particular section of society is shunned by decent folk in the city too."

"For associating with Lizzie?" I asked.

"Associating is perhaps a not strong enough word, if you know what I mean."

"I confess I am in the dark as to what you mean."

Holmes chuckled. "I believe Hogan is trying to tell you that it appears Lizzie's connections to these women would be termed by some unenlightened souls as unnatural."

I spluttered something I cannot recall, but I am confident my response would have been one of disbelief.

"Come now, Watson, you cannot surely be shocked, not a man of your wide experience. Women over three continents I believe you once informed me," Holmes said, playfully.

"That may be so, Holmes, well it is so, but I am not familiar with what I believe is termed Sapphic love."

"And as a burgeoning pillar of the establishment, you are disapproving."

"Neither statement is true. I do not disapprove nor do I approve particularly, I accept that it happens, but I do not dwell on it. I hope that answer will suffice, Holmes."

"Forgive me for traducing your ideals, my friend. Now, Hogan, have you any other news to share with us?"

"I spent part of the night of what turned out to be a very long day at Metacomet Mill questioning members of the dispatch department. I thought it would do no harm to check on Charlie Walter's story."

"Of necessity, it would be one of my first actions too if I were in charge of this case. What did you find?"

"The fact that Walters clocked in and out cannot be denied; that does not just rely on the evidence of his punching-in card, but also reliable witnesses who both saw and spoke to him as he performed both actions. No one is sure about exactly when they saw him throughout the night and I was told his usual activities chiefly consist of locking himself away in his office where most of the staff are loath to disturb him, particularly lately when it appears he has been like a bear with a sore head. Besides it was a very busy night with a lot of traffic entering and leaving the mill. The carts and wagons pass directly under Walters's office and one or two of the drivers reported seeing the back of his head as he leaned back from his desk. Nothing untoward or unexpected happened during the shift apart from a prank played on one the workers; it seems one of them complained bitterly halfway through his shift that his bicycle had been stolen, but it must been a joke played on him for when his shift ended, the bicycle was back in its usual position behind the dispatch area."

"We can dismiss Walters therefore as being involved in the murder of his wife." I stated.

"Do you think so, Watson?"

"I agree with the doctor, Mr Holmes, the eye-witness evidence precludes any view to the contrary."

"Ah well, if we look at the evidence from a different perspective then there could be a shifting of the sands and a different tale arises," said Holmes enigmatically. "Is there any news regarding Emma's return?"

"I have had a wire from her in reply to my own; she will be arriving back in Fall River late tomorrow morning."

"Excellent, we will look forward to making her acquaintance. I know your uncle is not, how shall we say, seeing eye to eye with me at the moment, but if you hold any sway with him, could you persuade him to remove the police presence at 'Maplecroft'?"

"I will undertake that myself if you consider it important."

"I do, but have no desire to place you in an awkward position, Hogan, but I believe such a move may well be beneficial."

"Without explaining why, Holmes?"

"You know my methods, Watson as does Hogan by now. I will keep my own counsel a while longer."

"I will see to it right away, Mr Holmes."

"Thank you, Hogan. One more thing, if we wished to gain admittance to 'Maplecroft' ourselves, would that be possible, later today for instance?"

"I will leave the rear door unlocked and God preserve me from the wrath of uncles! The housekeeper, Mrs Gray has decided that a couple of days off would benefit her and the other servants have been stood down for the time being until Emma's return."

"Oh and just in case your uncle has a change of heart regarding Lizzie's guilt and decides to release her, please impress on him the importance of not doing so, for if she is released in the next twenty-four hours then it is certain there will be another murder."

"Another murder? Who is the intended victim?" I asked.

"I have no idea, my dear fellow, but rest assured it will happen."

"I had a notion that you are far from convinced of Lizzie's guilt. Have you had a change of heart?"

"No, not at all. I remain unconvinced."

"But you seem to be implying that she will commit another murder if released, Mr Holmes."

"You saw it as that, did you? I see…well, we will liaise with you later, Hogan," said Holmes, dismissing him with a wave of his arm.

I endeavoured to draw Holmes further on his statement regarding a third murder, but to no avail.

"What are our plans today?" I asked as Hogan left.

"First, I think we will refresh our collective memories regarding the Borden case."

"I fear mine is in need of rather more refreshing than yours."

"Quite so! I believe we had reached the point of the trial taking place had we not? William Moody, who was appointed to head the prosecution by Arthur Pilsbury the Attorney General of Massachusetts, from all accounts, was the most competent attorney involved in the Borden trial. He was the most thorough in the questioning of witnesses. Knowlton, in contrast, would sometimes open a line of questioning and then walk away from it and Moody's arguments to the court about the admissibility of evidence were impressive, even if they failed to sway the three judges. His opening statement delineating the issues that the prosecution would bring to the demonstration of Lizzie's guilt were clear, firm, and logical."

"William Moody made the opening statements for the prosecution. He presented three arguments. First, Lizzie was predisposed to murder her father and stepmother and that she had planned it. Second, that she did in fact murder them, and, third, that her behaviour and contradictory testimony was not consistent with innocence. At one point, Moody threw a dress onto the prosecution table that he was to offer later in evidence. As the dress fell on the table, tissue paper covering the fleshless skulls of the victims was wafted away. Lizzie slid to the floor in a dead faint."

"Which one supposes would possibly have happened regardless of her guilt or innocence." I said.

"Quite possibly so. Crucial to the prosecution case was the presentation of evidence that supplied a motive for the murders, for without a semblance of a motive than the prosecution would surely fail. Fellow prosecutors Knowlton and Moody called witnesses to establish that Mr Borden was intending to write a new will. An old will was never found, or did not exist, although John Morse testified at first that Mr Borden had told him that he had a will. He then proceeded to testify that Mr Borden had not told him of a will, resulting in another instance of contradictions amongst the witnesses. The new will, according to Uncle John, would leave Emma and Lizzie each twenty-five thousand dollars, with the remainder of Mr. Borden's half million dollar estate going to Abby. Further, Knowlton developed the additional motive of Mr Borden's intent to dispose of his farm to Abby, just as he had done the year before with the duplex occupied by Abby's sister, Sarah Whitehead. Knowlton then turned to Lizzie's alleged predisposition towards murder. However, two rulings by the court were to prove crucial to Lizzie's eventual verdict of innocent."

"What were they?" I asked, interrupting Holmes's flow. "And may I say your memory for these details is nothing short of astounding."

"It is not such a prodigious feat as you imagine, Watson for I brought my copious notes on the case with me."

"But you could not have known of our involvement in this city beforehand."

"Indeed, no, but I had the notion of visiting Fall River and circumstances allowed that to happen in a way I had not expected."

"Quite so. The two rulings, however?"

"Ah, yes. On Saturday, June 10th, the prosecution attempted to enter Lizzie's testimony from the inquest into the record. Robinson objected, since it was testimony from one who had not been formally charged. On Monday, when court resumed, the justices disallowed the introduction of Lizzie's contradictory inquest testimony. On Wednesday, June 14th, the prosecution called Eli Bence, the drug store clerk, to the stand, and the defence objected. After hearing arguments from both the prosecution and the defence as to the relevance of Lizzie's attempt to purchase prussic acid, the justices ruled the following day that Mr. Bence's testimony and the entire issue of her alleged attempt to buy poison was irrelevant and inadmissible and therefore of course the testimony to come from Sansom Weinberger regarding Lizzie's approach to him, which was being kept in reserve, was also now worthless."

"The defence team which was chiefly Andrew Jennings and Melvin Adams worked successfully to exclude testimony that would have been damaging to Lizzie. For the most part, the defence called witnesses to verify the presence of a mysterious young man in the vicinity, although, not one was thoroughly convincing and Emma Borden to verify the absence of a motive for Lizzie as the murderer. Emma Borden, who we will meet tomorrow, is something of an enigma from all accounts. She is variously described as shy, retiring, small, plain looking, thin-faced and bony, quite an unremarkable forty-three-year-old spinster. The most well-known depiction of her is an unsatisfactory drawing made of her in court. She was supportive of Lizzie during the trial, although there is one witness, a prison matron, who testified that Lizzie and Emma had an argument when Emma was visiting her in jail. After the trial, she and Lizzie lived together at 'Maplecroft'. While Lizzie found it impossible to attend church following the trial, Emma, unlike her previous existence, became a devoted churchgoer."

"The third member of the defence team, George Robinson delivered the closing arguments and Knowlton began his closing arguments for the prosecution, completing them on the next day. Lizzie was then asked if she had anything to say. For the only time during the trial, she spoke. She said, "I am innocent. I leave it to my counsel to speak for me." Justice Dewey, who had been appointed to the Superior Court bench by the then Governor Robinson, delivered his charge to the jury, which was, in effect, a second summation of the case for the defence, remarkable in its bias. At 3:24, the jury was sworn, given the case, and retired to carry out their deliberations. At 4:32, a little over an hour later, the jury returned with its verdict. Lizzie was found not guilty on all three charges. The jury was earnestly thanked by the court, and dismissed."

"Officially, in spite of the rumours, the case remains unsolved?"

"Precisely. Can you be ready to leave in ten minutes, Watson?"

"I can be. Where are we going?"

"To North Main Street, to see Charlie Walters.

Emma Borden

Maplecroft

Chapter Eleven

The walk to North Main Street from Second Street occupied us for no more than ten minutes and during that time Holmes said nothing to me of why he wanted to see Mr Walters again. Instead, he chose to discourse on the origins of the city of Fall River; how it went by the name of Troy for some thirty years before returning to its original name of Fallriver, subtly changed however to become Fall River. The southern part of Fall River opted to split from the industrial north and became Tiverton, Rhode Island. At this time the northern part of Fall River was partly in Rhode Island too, but a Supreme Court decision in the 1860's placed the whole of Fall River in Massachusetts. By the time Holmes had come to the end of my history lesson we had arrived at Charlie Walters's apartment.

He hardly welcomed us with open arms, perhaps understandably in view of his recent, sudden loss.

"I am sorry to intrude on you at this time, but I wanted to keep you apprised on how the investigation into your wife's murder is progressing and I did have a question or two for you which slipped my mind yesterday."

"Very well, but keep it snappy," he growled.

"Lizzie Borden or Lizbeth as she calls herself now, is under lock and key and remains the only suspect. You are not aware of any other connection between your wife and Lizzie other than the attempted theft incident?"

"None at all, though there was bad feeling on my wife's part for some time; in fact she spoke to me once of going up to Lizzie's fine house up there on the Hill and having it out with her."

"Thank you. Chief Hogan is convinced Lizzie is the culprit and that is the feeling in the city too. Emma, Lizzie's sister is due back from a visit tomorrow morning and may yet be able to shed some light on the proceedings. The public have decided they have had enough of surrounding the Borden's house like a lynch mob and have dispersed. The Chief tells me that he will send a team into 'Maplecroft' tomorrow and begin a painstaking search of the house."

"But, Holmes…" I started.

Holmes silenced me with a glance.

"I am assured by Elmer Hogan that if there is any connection at all between Lizzie and the current murders then it will be found. Before we take our leave, Mr Walters, did your wife use a perfume by the name of 'Midnight in Paris'? The scent cropped up during the investigation into Sansom Weinberger's murder and I was intrigued as to whether it was a popular scent amongst the ladies of Fall River."

"My wife was in the habit of buying her own perfumes and trinkets, I was never a believer in such things."

"Perhaps you would permit me to make a brief search?"

"Allow me a few minutes to tidy up; I pride myself on being a perfect host in all circumstances," he said, somewhat incongruously in view of the chaotic state of the apartment.

Before Holmes could answer, Walters had left the room. We heard his footsteps racing around in, presumably, the bedroom and a few moments later he re-joined us. Holmes rose and made his way to the Walter's bedroom. His footsteps were more measured as I would have expected. When he came into the room, he looked at me and shook his head.

"Thank you, Mr Walters," he said, "you have been a great help. We will be in touch soon. Goodbye."

When we found ourselves on the pavement I asked Holmes about his pointedly false statement regarding the search of 'Maplecroft'.

"Sorry to cut you short there, Watson, but I had a very good reason for misleading Charlie Walters although it is entirely accurate to say there will be a search made tomorrow, but it will be made by us."

"I understood that is the reason for our visit to 'Maplecroft' today, Holmes."

"So it is, Watson, so it is."

"Am I being obtuse here? Would you care to explain this, what shall I say, strategy of yours?"

"Let us await further events for even now, I may be on the wrong scent altogether" he said, chuckling. "Now, the Borden's house is in Queen Street, on what is called The Hill. It's a fair step I believe, but as time is not pressing on us, shall we walk? Are you up to it, Watson?"

I assured him I was more than up to it and we set off at a reasonable pace which alas on my part, soon slowed.

'Maplecroft' was rather larger than I had imagined and as impressive as it was from the outside it did not prepare us for the lavishness of the interior. After admitting ourselves through the rear door which Hogan had left unlocked for us, we wandered through the house. There was a wealth of fine detail from Italian arches, stained-glass windows through to detailed mantles and beamed ceilings. There were six fireplaces throughout the house and three full baths and two half-baths. The billiard room was particularly impressive. The houses either side of the property, Holmes told me, had been purchased for the servants to reside in. Whatever else the murder of Andrew Borden had done, it had certainly made Lizzie a wealthy lady together with her sister. I assumed Holmes would know something of the matter of the will as he had intimated before and asked him.

"A thoughtful question, Watson. Abby's will consisted chiefly of donations to charity and if Andrew had pre-deceased her then his considerable fortune would have gone to her and thence, presumably to charity, notwithstanding family protests. Of course, Abby died first, albeit by a short time, and Andrew's money went to his two daughters."

"Thank you; tell me, what precisely are we searching for here?"

"We are looking for something that isn't here."

"That begs the question, just why are we here then?"

"I need to satisfy my curiosity and a theory that has formed itself. You know my methods; I do nothing without a reason."

We located Lizzie's suite of rooms, easily identifiable with Lizzie's monogrammed stationery sitting on both dressing-table and writing desk, and Holmes became more focused and intent. After a few minutes only, he declared himself satisfied.

"I take it the outcome of your search was exactly how you thought it would be."

"Indeed, Watson and I think we can now leave this place until our return to make the acquaintance of Emma Borden tomorrow."

"And our next move?"

"Let's see if we can find anything resembling a cup of tea anywhere in this city, I have my doubts however."

"Tea would be most welcome, that's for sure. How do we proceed with Emma Borden's request to look into the murders of Andrew and Abby Borden?"

"The records of the trial and preliminary hearings are available at City Hall and Elmer Hogan has also made the police records of the investigation available, but we will not trouble ourselves about that until we have spoken to Emma; tomorrow will be soon enough."

"Shall I secure the rear door, Holmes?"

"No, Watson, I am very keen for the door to remain unsecured. We will exit through the front door."

Charles and Honoria Walters

Chapter Twelve

Even Holmes's revered sleuthing skills were not enough to track down that elusive cup of tea so we both settled for particularly and perhaps unnecessarily strong coffees. As we drank them I drew him out on the events of the day.

"You, to my mind, obviously suspect Charlie Walters of the murder of his wife although I fail to see what has led you to that conclusion, and where does the murder of Sansom Weinberger fit into this scenario of yours?"

"There was something in his manner which did not ring true. When we spoke to him he was almost confrontational and his gestures spoke to me of a man who was lying."

"He had just discovered his wife brutally murdered, you can hardly expect the man to act normally under the circumstances and his gestures, however you saw them, may be just be characteristics of the man."

"I beg to differ, Watson. I had no time to dwell on it because we were then driven to the site of the second murder of the day. The scent that I came across in Weinberger's apartment that reminded me of 'The Seine by Moonlight' made me realise that I had caught a trace of it earlier at the Walters's apartment. The knowledge we gained later that Sansom Weinberger and Honoria Walters knew each other had the result of pointing me in a definite direction."

"There is no indication as to how well they knew each other. All we know is that they met at Chamber of Commerce meetings and recently they have not even attended the same meetings."

"Perhaps deliberately so to avoid any gossip, Watson. Somehow, I think Charlie Walters got wind of what was happening and was determined to put a stop to the relationship, not being the kind of man to sit back and do nothing. He may have hoped to catch his wife and Weinberger together. Perhaps, to be fair to the man, he merely wanted to warn them although the presence of the axe tends to outweigh that consideration."

"But why would Weinberger admit the man?"

"I think it entirely possible that Honoria Walters knocked Weinberger's door in a certain way so he would know it was her, such coded messages are popular in clandestine relationships it seems although my knowledge of romance is somewhat limited. If Walters had followed his wife previously then he may have observed this procedure and duplicated it. Admittedly, this is speculation and I can think of five other theories that would cover the matter."

"But he was at the mill all night, there are witnesses who saw him there and there is the small matter of him clocking in and clocking out, Holmes."

"The fact that he was registered entering the mill and leaving at the end of the shift does not mean he was actively on the premises at all times. Remember, he was in the habit of locking himself away in his office and would not be disturbed for hours at a time. And you no doubt recall the worker whose bicycle went missing…"

"I see now. Walters slipped out unnoticed. He was surely taking a risk though?"

"To our minds yes, not to his though. Having disposed of Weinberger he went to his own apartment. No doubt he had his key with him, but knocked the door to bring his wife down to him, thereby making it look as though someone else had come to the door. I believe he struck her down as soon as she opened the door and showed her absolutely no mercy."

"And he hoped to get away with it by implicating Lizzie Borden?"

"Indeed, Watson for he would have known of the incident involving his wife and the fact that Lizzie had tried to purchase poison from Weinberger was no doubt well known in Fall River society circles."

"How could he be sure that Lizzie would not have an alibi?"

"I think he had slipped away from the mill on previous occasions and knew about Lizzie's nocturnal wanderings. He may have known that Emma was away. In fact, I think it is certain he knew hence the timing of his crime. He is a cold-blooded killer and tomorrow I have no doubt he will fall into the trap I have laid for him."

"You expect him to gain entrance to 'Maplecroft' and plant a bottle of 'Midnight in Paris' there."

"Quite so. He wants to try by some means to make the case against Lizzie a little stronger. It will be his undoing."

"You mentioned the likelihood of another murder should Elmer Hogan release Lizzie…"

"I believe that if she was no longer a suspect then Walters would take even more desperate steps to ensure that she remained one, a murder of someone connected with her; for instance someone at Tilden-Thurber Art Gallery in Providence where she was accused of stealing two pictures earlier this year."

"Would Walters have known of this?"

"It was published in the Providence Journal and we can be reasonably sure that Honoria Walters would have known of it. We cannot exclude the fact that he had plans, if all else failed, to strike at someone very close to Lizzie."

"Emma?"

"He would be desperate enough to do so, but the opportunity will be denied to him. We will ensure that, my friend."

The rest of the day was spent in wandering around Fall River as though we were tourists with time on our hands. In spite of the industrial nature of the city, it did have a beauty of its own with a recognisable heartbeat in which industry and ordinary everyday life came together in unity. Prosperity was the byword here.

Chapter Thirteen

After breakfasting very well indeed, Peter Jubb proving to be more than equal to the task of supplying sustenance to his two English guests, we prepared ourselves for our impending visit to 'Maplecroft'. This visit, of course, would be a legitimate one as opposed to our visit of the day before. The sun was high and the heat of the day was already apparent and the temperature was set to rise steeply. The Borden murders had been committed on just such a stiflingly hot morning and the proximity of the Borden house had triggered a train of thoughts in my head. Would it be, that even Holmes with all his deductive skills and experience would fail to unravel the truth of what occurred five years previously? Would the truth, indeed, ever be known?

Given our experience in interviewing Lizzie Borden, we could not expect to learn the truth, whatever that may be, from that quarter. Whatever she knew or did not know was locked up inside her. Wishing for some fresher air although not confident of finding any, I went out onto the porch while Holmes was involved in a debate with Jubb, the nature of which I did not really understand fully. Mr O' Hara was also taking some air and we exchanged cordial greetings. The air was still and oppressive.

"Could be a storm heading our way, Dr Watson."

"I shouldn't wonder at it, Mr O'Hara."

"It was a morning such as this when the murders took place."

"I am aware and in fact that thought was uppermost in my mind just prior to coming out here. I was wondering, among other things, how it must have felt that morning in the house."

"I can help you there. Be my guest and come and see for yourself."

I stepped across to the Borden house and entered.

"Doors all shut and windows closed, just how it was that day. Feel free to wander."

The room where Andrew Borden met his end was already unbearably hot and I imagined how easy it would have been for him to enter the room on returning home after concluding his business for the day and being overcome with a need to sleep. Although I was refreshed by a good night's slumber I felt I could quite easily fall into a deep sleep.

The guest room where Abby had been surprised as she stripped the bed that John Morse had slept in was no less unbearable. As I tried to imagine the unspeakable violence done to her and what thoughts she had, if any, when the first blow struck her I felt not just the oppressiveness of the morning sun as the mercury rose, but also the very oppressiveness of the house and the room. And there was something more that I have never really been able to put into words to my own satisfaction. I cannot recall when I left the room or how long I was in there. Clear to me is Mr O'Hara's face and look of bemusement as I passed him in the hall without a word and made my way back to Jubb's house.

"Whatever is the matter, Watson? You look as though you have seen a ghost."

"Well," I replied. "I am not a fanciful man as you know and I certainly cannot tell you I have seen or heard anything next door to make me so, but come hell or high water, I am never going back in that house, Holmes."

"It may have only been five years since the murders, but already the house has acquired a certain reputation," Jubb said.

Holmes poured scorn on such talk, believing imagination to be at work with those who may have claimed to have had such experiences, myself included. Perhaps he was right, yet my resolve not to enter the Borden house again was just as strong.

Thirty minutes later we were on our way up to the Hill once more where Emma Borden would be waiting for us. Holmes assured me that young Hogan was going to meet her and give her all the information he could about her sister's incarceration and his hopes that she would be released in due course.

The housekeeper, who introduced herself as Mrs Courtenay Gray, admitted us and took our coats and hats. She silently showed us into a large sitting-room which we were familiar with and there perched on the sofa was Emma and seated in two large armchairs either side of her were Elmer and Michael Hogan.

"Good morning, Mr Holmes and Dr Watson, nice to meet you. Tell me, Mr Holmes, my kin folk here have been favouring me with their views regarding my sister's guilt or innocence, tell me straight then, what do you say?"

"Miss Borden…" started Holmes.

"Mr Holmes has no official standing here, Emma and this investigation has to be carried out according to facts and evidence, not one man's thoughts."

"Why, Elmer, why do you always think the worst of Lizzie? You would love her to be guilty and I never knew why, nor do I know now."

"I am a policeman, Emma. I am doing my job, that's all."

"Michael is a policeman too yet he seems to have more empathy than you. Mr Holmes, I am sorry, we have interrupted you."

"Miss Borden, I am convinced of your sister's innocence. With your permission, I would like to go to your sister's room."

"For what purpose?"

"To clear your sister's name," Holmes replied as he made for the stairs.

If Emma was in anyway surprised by this she did not betray it on her features. Taller than her sister, with sharply defined cheekbones and a prominent chin, she shared with Lizzie an inscrutable look and once more I had the feeling, as I did with Lizzie, that she was capable of anything if she put her mind to it.

"Gentlemen," Holmes announced as he returned to the room, holding up a small bottle, "'Midnight in Paris', it was sitting on Lizzie's dressing-table."

"That clinches it then," said Chief Hogan. "Although I am surprised it was not found by my own men."

"Yes it does and I am not surprised at all," said Holmes.

"That cannot be Lizzie's, she does not use scent of any kind."

"You are right, Miss Borden, for this perfume only entered the house overnight."

"Explain yourself, Mr Holmes."

"Certainly, Chief Hogan."

Holmes went on to explain the events of the previous day and notwithstanding several black looks shot at the younger Hogan from the elder Hogan, the Chief accepted Holmes's version of events and both Hogans departed to arrest Charlie Walters.

"Walters, as we thought, could not resist the chance to provide some material evidence to heighten the police suspicions. He is a heartless man who deserves no mercy from any quarter. Once Walters is under lock and key, then I have no doubt Michael will bring your sister home, Miss Borden."

"I am glad to hear it, Mr Holmes. Now, are you prepared to look into the slaying of my father and step-mother?"

"That is why we have come to Fall River, but you must understand that there is no guarantee that the truth, should I discover it, will be favourable to you. Indeed, it may be the case that this crime will ever remain unsolved, after all it is five years now and witnesses may have moved on, evidence lost. I will have access to all the notes that the local police have in their file. I will have access too to the court transcripts and full records pertaining to the premlinary hearings."

"You have a lot of ground to cover, but that is good, for surely the answer lies in there somewhere."

"It may not, Miss Borden, that is my point. With all that, it may not be enough."

"I will put my trust in your abilities and that of your colleague here."

"Thank you. It may be necessary to come back after sifting through all these files and ask you some painful, but relevant questions. The same stricture will apply to Lizzie too."

"I do not foresee a problem with that although I cannot vouch for my sister; it is a topic she never raises or discusses and Lord knows I have tried, oh so many times."

"If we can spare you both then we will. We will leave you to prepare a welcome for your sister and we will go and begin our task."

Emma rang a small bell and Mrs Courtenay Gray glided noiselessly into the room with our hats and coats and showed us to the door.

"Watson, if you wish to spend your time away from the confines of dusty files and weighty paperwork, then you must be at your ease to say so. It is an onerous task, but it is one I can accomplish alone."

"*Best* accomplished alone perhaps?"

"That was not my meaning. You will be of the greatest help to me; your insights are often illuminating and occasionally pertinacious in the extreme."

"I believe you flatter me, Holmes, but you can count me in."

"Ah, I know my Watson. I think we will start at the beginning and start with the files that the police hold. We'll pay a visit to the Chief who by now should be enjoying the accolades being poured on him by Marshal Rufus B. Hilliard for his apprehension of Fall River's double killer."

MARSHAL HILLIARD.

Chapter Fourteen

Elmer Hogan, smiling, with an arm stretched out, greeted us in his office.

"Thank you, Mr Holmes. I fear I have been guilty of being blinkered in my pursuit of the truth in this case and had I not had you to show me the light, my career might have suffered irreparably."

I was a little indignant when hearing this statement. "Do not forget sir, there was more than your career to think of; you may have incarcerated an innocent woman and no matter what feelings you have on the events of five years ago, the simple truth that the people of this city forget is that Lizzie was cleared of all charges and surely she has the right available to any other citizen to be adjudged innocent until proven guilty. Is she to be suspected of every heinous crime that occurs in Fall River?"

"I am not accustomed to being browbeaten in my own office, Dr Watson and the simple truth that you fail to grasp is that Lizzie, and it pains me to say it as she is kin, was undoubtedly guilty of the crimes she was charged with and I am not the arbiter of other people's feelings; they call it as they see it, but you won't find many in this city subscribing to the view of an innocent Lizzie Borden."

"I think it is maybe time to begin our inspection of the files, Watson," interjected Holmes.

"I have laid everything out for you in a small room at the rear of the storage area on the third floor. If there is anything else you need, please ask."

"Thank you, Chief."

The room we had been allocated was dimly lit, but sufficient for our needs. The huge mass of paperwork had been unceremoniously thrown on to the rickety table and it became clear that there was no logical or chronological order to the files. The order would have to come from us. To that end, we set about sifting what we could and placing it into some semblance of order.

"Surely, Holmes, you already have most of this information in your own folder of papers pertaining to the case."

"Some, but not all and it is most informative to see the original hand-written notes, they tell us so much more that what has merely been written."

"There is certainly an abundance of those notes here!"

"We can apportion some of the blame to Marshal Hilliard for he insisted that any officer who had been present and any officers who had a clue of any kind should write up a minutely detailed report to be laid at his door for examination; these would then be forwarded to the District Attorney. Ah, here is an interesting thing," he said, holding up a note with a torn edge.

"What is it?"

"It's written by the officer, Sergeant Harrington, who examined the loft. Lizzie's story, or at least one of them, was that after her father came home she went up into the loft of the barn to look for lead sinkers. The officer also went to the loft. It was covered with dust and there were no tracks to prove that any person had been there for weeks. He took particular notice of the fact, and reported back that he had walked about on the dust-covered floor on purpose to discover whether or not his own feet left any tracks. He writes here that they did and thinks it singular that anybody could have visited the floor a short time before him and made no impressions on the dust. The lower floor of the stable told no such tale, as it was evident that it had been used more frequently and the dust had not accumulated there. The conclusion reached was that in the excitement incident to the awful discovery, Miss Borden had forgotten just where she went for the lead."

"But this is information you already have."

"Quite so, but it is rather pleasing to have it from the horse's mouth so to speak."

We continued our sifting in this room where the daylight could not penetrate. Occasionally Holmes would break the silence with a sudden shout of exclamation. It was over an hour before we concluded we had all the papers in a semblance of chronological order. I disappeared in search of a coffee whilst Holmes began his examination in earnest. When I returned, Holmes was sitting immobile, smoking his pipe, the room wreathed in impenetrable smoke.

"If you would be so kind, Watson, we will begin with the officer's statements of that morning. If anything strikes you as worthy of note, disturb my thoughts and we will look at it together. The starting point are the notes of Officer George Allen, if you will permit me to read them out loud; *'Fifteen minutes past eleven A. M. the Marshal came out of his office and said "Mr. Allen, I want you to go up on Second street, the house next to Mrs. Buffington's above Borden street, and see what the matter is." I ran out of the station up Second Street, and just before I got to Mr. Borden's house I met Mr. Sawyer. I told him I wanted him to go with me; and he went. When I got to the side door of Mr. Borden's house, I was met by Dr. Bowen. He said he wanted a police officer. Mr. Sawyer said I was one. He said "all right, come right in." I told Mr. Sawyer to guard the side door, and not allow anyone to come in, only police officers. Dr. Bowen took me into the sitting room where Mr. Borden lay. He was on the lounge with his face turned upwards. Several cuts long and deep on the left side of the face. Doctor said "you go down, and tell the Marshal all about it." I ran down to the station as fast as I could go, and told the Marshal that Mr. Borden had been cut in the face with something like a razor. He said "is he dead"? I told him he was. He gave me orders to go and find Officer Mullally, which I did in a few minutes, and brought him to the station. The Marshal gave him orders to go right up to Mr. Borden's house. He was there by twenty five minutes past eleven o'clock A. M. Just before we got there, Officer Doherty was ahead of us. When we went upstairs the Doctor said Mrs. Borden had fainted with fright. Officers Mullaly and Doherty turned her over. Officer Doherty said "My God her face is all smashed in." I went back to the station, and reported to the Marshal, and he went out, and went up that way'.*"

"Seems a peculiar thing for the doctor to say; surely he knew Abby Borden was dead at first glance."

"It was certainly odd, Watson. What have you there?" he asked as I pointed to a line in the statement in front of me."

"This is from Officer Harrington again, he has written; *'Lizzie stood by the foot of the bed, and talked in the most calm and collected manner; her whole bearing was most remarkable under the circumstances. There was not the least indication of agitation. No sign of sorrow or grief, no lamentation of the heart, no comment on the horror of the crime, and no expression of a wish that the criminal be caught. All this, and something that, to me, is indescribable, gave birth to a thought that was most revolting. I thought, at least, she knew more than she wished to tell.*' This took place in Lizzie's room which was being searched at the time."

"Harrington was suspicious of Lizzie almost as soon as he arrived at the Borden house it seems."

"Yes, Holmes, he goes on to write, let me see now, oh yes here it is; '*I then went to the Borden barn, where the Marshal gave orders to several officers to search the barn thoroughly, and took part in the work down stairs. It was at this time I made known my suspicions of Miss Lizzie. To the Marshal I said "I don't like that girl". He said "what is that?" I repeated, and further said "under the circumstances she does not act in a manner to suit me; it is strange, to say the least." When we finished the first floor of the barn, we ascended to the loft, the Marshal going just ahead of me. There I found officers Conners, Doherty and J. Riley. The Marshal said, "I want you men to go give this place a complete going over; every nook and corner must be looked into, and this hay turned over." I then said to him "if any girl can show you or me, or anybody else what could interest her up here for twenty minutes, I would like to have her do it." The Marshal shook his head, and said something about it being incredible; his words I cannot give. He assisted in the search for some minutes, and then went downstairs. I remained until we were satisfied our duty was done.*'

"I have here the witness statements collected by various officers. All of them are agreed on one point, there were no strangers to be seen either at the front of the house or the rear yard."

"How busy would it have been on the street? Could these witnesses have missed something?"

"It was then as it is now, a mix of domesticity and industry, the Fall River Ice Company was just south of the house for instance, and consequently a busy street particularly in the mornings. Due in part to these statements and to the intuition of officers such as Harrington, the Fall River police quickly came to hold the view that the murders must have been committed by someone in the house and suspicion could only fall on Bridget Sullivan and Lizzie Borden. A few snippets should suffice for our needs; ....*Afterwards Dr.Collet's daughter Lucy was sent up to Dr. Chagnon's to await callers. She could not gain entrance, for the door was locked, so she remained in the yard from 9.45 A. M., or thereabouts, to 12 M, when the assistant returned. She is positive no one could go through the yard without being seen by her. She heard no noise. The next yard contains a barn, and is occupied by John Crowe, a mason and builder. On the day in question John Denny, a stone cutter, employed by Mr. Crowe, was working in there all day. He is positive no one went through the yard. There were other men drawing stone to the yard all day, and they saw nothing of any suspicious character. Patrick McGowan is the man who was eating pears on the pile of lumber, and said to have been on the fence. He is employed by Mr. Crowe, and left the yard about 10. A. M. The next house is occupied by Mrs. Crapo. She and the girl were at home all Thursday August 4th, but heard no noise; neither did they see any person go through their yard. The Fall River Ice Co. is next South; and in this yard there are several men constantly employed. We saw them, and they reported nobody came their way. In the morning, shortly before the murder, Dr. Kelly's girl, Mary, was talking to Bridget over the fence, neither saw anyone in or around the yard. On this morning Mrs. Dr. Bowen was sitting at her front window, which is directly opposite the Borden yard, and in full view of both front and side doors, awaiting and watching for the coming of her daughter. She was at this window until 10.55 A. M. The daughter was away, and was expected on the forenoon train. At this point Mrs. Bowen arose, and said "well, she will not come now." Mrs. Churchill left her house about 11. A. M. and returned between 11.15 and 11.20. While away her mother, Mrs. Buffington, was in the dining room off the kitchen, wheeling to and fro a baby carriage which contained a sick baby; and although the windows were open, she heard no noise. Mrs. John Gomeley was in her room at No. 90 Second street, window open, heard no noise, saw no one. At 11.15 A. M. Dennis Sullivan, employed at Allen & Slades, came along and stopped to talk to Mrs. Gomeley. While going up Second street he saw no person leave the yard or go up or down the street on whom he could place suspicion.*'

"Other statements serve to reinforce the view that no one could have approached the Borden house from the rear. The testimonies of those on Second Street tell a similar story as regards the front of the property."

"Ah, what have we here?"

"What have you found, Watson?"

"Another observation by Officer Harrington, he writes of Lizzie's concern for her father; *When the perpetrator of this foul deed is found, it will be one of the household. I had a long talk with Lizzie yesterday, Thursday, the day of the murder, and I am not at all satisfied with her statement or demeanour. She was too solicitous about his comfort, and showed a side of character I never knew or even suspected her to possess. She helped him off with one coat and on with another, and assisted him in an easy incline on the sofa, and desired to place an afghan over him, and also to adjust the shutters so the light would not disturb his slumber. This is something she could not do, even if she felt; and no one who knows her, could be made to believe it. She is very strong willed, and will fight for what she considers her rights.*' He obviously knew Lizzie fairly well."

"Indeed and as such, he makes for a good witness to her character."

As each note had been read we transferred them to a pile stacked on the right-hand side of the table. My head had been swimming for the previous hour when Holmes declared we had seen enough in the copious files, much of it both contradictory and informative. Even allowing for contradictions, there seemed to be no doubt, as Holmes had expressed earlier that the murderer had to be someone in the house. The medical testimony we examined was categorically of the opinion that Abby Borden was killed first. The death of Andrew Borden came anything up to ninety minutes later. Holmes was a little scathing of the methods that the medicos utilised to make this calculation, but all the same he was in general agreement that Abby had been murdered first with Andrew's following on some time later, possibly as long as ninety minutes, but equally possibly only an hour later or even less. The point of course there is that any killer would risk discovery while waiting to dispatch his second victim, an unlikely scenario, but one that must reflect in some way the truth of the matter.

"I fear we may be too late for the stolid folk of City Hall, Watson so I propose a fresh start in the morning. Are you in need of some refreshment, old fellow?"

"Most certainly."

"Excellent, I noted an intriguing looking Portuguese restaurant on Pleasant Street earlier, shall we go and investigate?"

I was none too sure exactly what a Portuguese menu would consist of, but any fears were out-voted by my hunger pangs which demanded they be assuaged as soon as possible.

"Very well, Holmes, lead me to it."

The Fall River Court House

Chapter Fifteen

The heat of the previous two days was paying us a farewell with heavy thunderstorms during the night which certainly would have kept me from sleeping had not the Portuguese meal already done so, assaulting my digestive system in a particularly violent manner. I did not want to appear discourteous so I made my way gingerly through Mr Jubb's breakfast as Holmes chuckled at my discomfort."

"Your experience of women over three continents is one thing, Watson, but your experience of dining appears to be less comprehensive."

"I fear I have to agree with you, Holmes. I think I will seek out different fare this evening."

"If you feel you are unequal to the task today then you must say so."

"I am more than equal, in fact I think the breakfast may have done me some good," I answered, not very convincingly.

"Excellent. It will, I'm afraid, be a very dull day. The transcripts of the inquests and the trial will be informative no doubt, but not exciting you understand."

"I am fully aware of that, Holmes."

"As soon as you declare yourself ready we shall begin our day in earnest."

Ten minutes later we were walking down Second Street in somewhat fresher, but more comfortable air. We could hear the Quequechan River, swollen by the overnight rain, rushing towards Mount Hope Bay. There were pedestrians a-plenty which only served to reinforce the view that five years ago, gaining access to the Borden house without being seen would be well-nigh impossible. Neighbours had been able to give reliable times for Andrew Borden leaving the house and returning. John Morse, too, was spotted as he left the house to go visiting. Bridget Sullivan had been seen washing the windows. It was not a street where you could remain unnoticed for very long.

"Holmes," I asked, "are you convinced of Lizzie's guilt? If so, have you always been so?"

"In spite of my leaning that way, I have always endeavoured to keep an open mind on the subject. That is why the chance to see all this first-hand material is so enlightening. That is not to say it will change my mind, but it may give pause for thought. As it stands, all the evidence points to Bridget and Lizzie being the only ones inside the house, alive that is."

"It would be difficult to ascribe a motive to the maid surely."

"The notion has been put forward that Bridget was unduly upset at being asked to wash the windows on such a hot day and reacted violently against Abby. It is hard to subscribe to such a view. If Bridget had murdered Abby, I believe her first instinct would be to flee, appalled at what she had done. To imagine her then calmly going about her work and slaughtering Andrew Borden on his return is ridiculous don't you think?"

"It seems rather unlikely."

"I think we can express it in stronger terms than that, Watson, it is impossible that she would behave in such a manner."

"Then we are left with Lizzie."

"Indeed, Watson, although some have suggested a certain amount of collusion between Lizzie and Bridget, believing there to be rather more familiarity between them than is usual between a maid and family member. In short, a relationship has been put forward."

"What is your view?"

"I discount any collusion on their part, had there been such collusion than one would expect their testimonies to dovetail perfectly, which they don't, although admittedly neither woman accused the other."

"We are once more left with Lizzie then."

Holmes nodded and we walked on in silence. We gave our names to a uniformed man on duty at the front desk of the City Hall. He passed our names to a young man standing nearby who seemed to be there for the express purpose of taking messages. He scurried out of view and came back a few moments later with an older man who walked toward us hurriedly, but with an embossed walking-stick which tapped out a staccato rhythm on the highly-polished tiled floor.

"Good morning, gentlemen. I am Daniel Andriacco, the senior archivist here. I have a copy of a request given to me by Elmer Hogan, authorised by Rufus B Hilliard and I have collected all the papers you will need in reference to the inquests into the death of Andrew and Abby Borden together with the transcripts of the subsequent trial. None of these papers must leave the building for any reason whatsoever, I trust you understand."

"Perfectly, Mr Andriacco," replied Holmes.

"Very well, follow me please."

We followed him into what appeared to be the very bowels of the building. The click-click of his walking-stick echoed down the endless line of corridors we walked down until at last we had reached our destination.

"Here we are, gentlemen," Andriacco said, unlocking a door. "It's not the largest or brightest room we have available, but it will have to suffice for your needs. When you finish, please put all the papers in order, lock the room and bring the key to whoever is manning the front desk."

Holmes assured him that is precisely what we would do and as Andriacco left the room, we settled down to our task.

"With what we gleaned yesterday and now coupled with these thorough accounts, we should be able to produce a comprehensive and definitive timetable of the events of that August day."

"I have been thinking…"

"Excellent, Watson, I have long recommended it to you as a course of action!"

I ignored Holmes's barb and continued. "The outlandish notion that Bridget could have murdered Abby and then gone calmly about her work, which you described as impossible, would surely apply to Lizzie too."

"There is a difference however in intent if not execution. Lizzie's savage attack on Abby, if we subscribe to the view of her as the perpetrator, although frenzied would have been planned. That is not to say, meticulous in its planning, but borne out of circumstances. We can perhaps surmise that Andrew Borden was planning to change his will, something that Abby was desirous of him doing. Perhaps he informed Lizzie of his intentions. If this change was imminent then a clear motive reveals itself. This was a crime of hate and greed and premeditated. And of course Abby had to die first."

"Why, Holmes?"

"If Andrew Borden were to die first, his considerable fortune would pass to his wife, no matter that she herself would die shortly afterwards. In the eyes of the law, Andrew's considerable fortune was now Abby's, to be disposed of under the terms of her will and if no such provision had been made, to Abby's living relatives. So, Abby had to die first."

"If it happened along those lines."

"It is just a surmise, but an informed one. Theories abound in this case, Watson. It has been suggested that Lizzie was in the grip of an epileptic fit when she murdered Abby and would consequently have no recall of the event."

"It is not outside the laws of probability, Holmes."

"What I see as probable and what you see are completely different things."

"I was not suggesting it was probable in this particular instance, but rather as a general observation."

"I am gratified to hear it for it would be odd indeed for Lizzie to suffer a fit just when she happened to have an axe in her hand and then, wonder of wonders, to suffer another one when her father came home."

"Well, when you put it like that, Holmes."

"Quite. Shall we make a start?"

The transcripts were arranged in date and time order so there was to be no laborious sifting and arranging to be done. We put each sheet of foolscap between us and commenced reading, starting with Lizzie's testimony at the inquest. I whistled and exclaimed, "Do you see there, Holmes?"

"I fear you are ahead of me."

"Here," I pointed.

Q. Besides that, do you know of anybody that your father had bad feelings toward or who had bad feelings toward your father?
A. I know of one man who has not been friendly with him. They have not been friendly for years.
Q. Who?

A. Mr. Hiram C. Harrington.
Q. What relation is he to him?
A. He is my father's brother-in-law.
Q. Your mother's brother?

> "Officer Harrington was related to the Bordens, well, well. I wonder if he had an axe to grind."
> "An unfortunate choice of words, Holmes," I said, smiling.
> "I find this just as interesting," said Holmes.

Q. Did you ever deed him any property?
A. He gave us, some years ago, Grandfather Borden's house on Ferry Street and he bought that back from us some weeks ago. I don't know just how many.
Q. As near as you can recall.
A. Well, I should say in June, but I am not sure.
Q. What do you mean by 'bought it back'?
A. He bought it off us and gave us the money for it.
Q. How much was it?
A. How much money? He gave us $5,000 for it.
Q. Did you pay him anything when you took a deed from him?
A. Pay him anything? No sir.
Q. How long ago was it you took a deed from him?
A. When he gave it to us?
Q. Yes.
A. I can't tell you. I should think five years.
Q. Did you have any other business transactions with him besides that?
A. No sir.
Q. In real estate?
A. No sir.
Q. Or in personal property?
A. No sir.
Q. Never?
A. Never.
Q. No transfer of property one way or another?
A. No sir.
Q. At no time?

A. No sir.
Q. And I understand he paid you the cash for this property?
A. Yes sir.
Q. You and Emma equally?
A. Yes sir.

"Coming so close to the killings makes this very pertinent. It may be an indication that Andrew was planning to change his will and this was a way of 'paying off' his daughters so to speak. As you no doubt noticed, Lizzie claimed to know nothing of her father's will."

"Why, assuming he did, would he tell Lizzie of an impending change in his will and not Emma as the older daughter?"

"Emma was away in Fairhaven at the time and perhaps he did not want to communicate such news by letter, so he told Lizzie in person as she was on the spot so to speak."

"I see here that Lizzie claimed not to know her father was dead when she saw him in the sitting-room," I said.

Q. Did you notice that he was dead?
A. I did not know whether he was or not.

"And again here."

Q. What did you tell Maggie?
A. I told her he was hurt.
Q. When you first told her?
A. I says, "Go for Dr. Bowen as soon as you can. I think father is hurt."
Q. Did you then know that he was dead?
A. No sir.

Holmes picked up the pile of notes pertaining to the trial itself and turned to Bridget Sullivan's testimony. "Bridget remembers it differently."

'The next thing was that Miss Lizzie hollered, "Maggie, come down!" I said, "What is the matter?" She says, "Come down quick; Father's dead; somebody came in and killed him." This might be ten or fifteen minutes after the clock struck eleven, as far as I can judge'.

"She is quite adamant on the subject of the note that Lizzie says came for Mrs Borden."

Q. You simply say that you didn't see anybody come with a note?
A. No sir, I did not.
Q. Easy enough for anybody to come with a note to the house, and you not know it, wasn't it?
A. Well, I don't know if a note came to the back door that I wouldn't know.
Q. But they wouldn't necessarily go to the back door, would they?
A. No. I never heard anything about a note, whether they got it or not. I don't know.
Q. Don't know anything about it, and so you don't undertake to say it wasn't there?
A. No sir.

"And earlier…"

Q. Up to the time when Miss Lizzie Borden told her father and told you in reference to the note, had you heard anything about it from anyone?
A. No sir, I never did.
Q. Let me ask you if anyone to your knowledge came to that house on the morning of August 4th with a message or a note for Mrs. Borden?
A. No sir, I never seen nobody.

"The note was an invention?"
"Perhaps if I express it thus, Watson. The only information regarding Abby Borden receiving a note came from Lizzie. A note was never found. No one ever came forward to say they were expecting a visit from Abby. In spite of the publicity, no one ever came forward to claim authorship of any note."
"That seems fairly conclusive, Holmes."
"If not conclusive then certainly suspicious."

We ploughed our way through sheaf after sheaf in pursuit of clarity and exactness. The medical testimony was in general agreement that death had come to Abby first. Each of the victims had been struck between twelve and nineteen blows of great savagery. The authorities were undecided on whether the hatchet found in the cellar with its handle broken was in fact the murder weapon although the wounds would suggest it was. The verdict of not guilty that the jury brought in was in fact the only verdict they could have formulated given the state of the evidence against Lizzie; there was no physical evidence linking her to either murder, no blood on her clothing or hands, nothing to link her to the hatchet and no clear motive.

As we left the room having called Mr Andriacco, I asked Holmes the question I could no longer put off asking.

"What will you tell Emma?"

"I will tell her the data I have seen is insufficient for me to to come to any decision regarding her sister's guilt or innocence."

"Emma is not a stupid woman, Holmes, she will see straight through you. If you believe, which I know you do, that Lizzie was guilty, wouldn't it be kinder to tell Emma that fact?"

"In her heart of hearts perhaps she has formed that opinion herself. If so, my words will make very little difference."

"But you are here at her request, Holmes. It's the truth she needs."

"As to that, who really knows the truth of what happened that day? One person only. On this occasion, I will not play God. After all, is my truth the truth? Is Lizzie's?"

"Dammit all, Holmes, Emma could be in danger."

"I do not think so; there is an alliance in that house, a house of secrets. No, Watson, my mind is made up. Tomorrow, we will see Emma and then set about booking our passage back to New York."

"You do not wish to stay on?"

"There is nothing here for me."

Holmes remained in a sombre mood for the rest of the day and could not be persuaded to dine. I smoked a pipe or two with Mr Jubb before retiring. I found that sleep eluded me and I spent a wakeful hour or two staring out of the window at the old Borden house. Whatever secrets it had once held were now in residence at 'Maplecroft' where they would remain. Holmes had spoken accurately; the truth of that scorching hot August day would never be known. We would leave the Borden sisters to their lives together.

Andrew Borden's body.

Abby Borden's body.

$5,000 REWARD!

The above Reward will be paid to any one who may secure the

Arrest and Conviction

of the person or persons, who occasioned the death of

Mr. Andrew J. Borden and Wife.

**EMMA J. BORDEN,
LIZZIE A. BORDEN.**

Chapter Sixteen

Before we departed Second Street for Queen Street the following morning, I stood on the porch steps and contemplated the Borden house one more time. I imagined it would be a house that would occur in my dreams hereafter, a place I would never entirely be free of.

Holmes joined me, placing a comforting hand on my shoulder.

"A house of barriers and locks, Watson, a house of distrust. Is it any wonder that such a tragedy occurred there? Andrew Borden, for all his wealth, was a miserly man and unloved too I believe. The locks on all the doors reflected perfectly the dysfunctional familial relationships. Lizzie's strained relationship with her father for instance and her open hostility towards her stepmother, admittedly not always open, but you suspect was always there."

We fell into step together and Holmes continued his narrative.

"As we surmised the number of suspects was very limited indeed, namely Bridget and Lizzie for the notion of anyone else being in the house be they stranger or family member must be accounted impossible. Lizzie claimed to have been in the kitchen around the time of her stepmother's murder yet heard nothing as a very heavy woman was viciously attacked and fell to the floor."

"But the maid heard nothing either, Holmes."

"True, but she was busy washing the windows, one supposes Lizzie chose her time well."

"There was no blood found on her dress, remember."

"Had the search been carried out by women then one may have been found. I believe the dress she wore was placed back in her wardrobe with another over the top of it. A remarkably simple strategy, but effective."

"Did she change twice then, once after each murder?"

"I do not think it was necessary, maybe not even after the first murder. There were few blood splashes at either crime scene. It may be that she was able to out a cotton wrapper over the dress she wore in the morning. Now, you saw the sitting-room where Andrew was murdered; the position of the sofa is such that you could strike a man laid on it without entering the room, at least for the initial blow, the fatal blow."

"Would Lizzie have the strength to carry out such an act?"

"You have met her so I believe you know the answer to that. She is as resolute a woman as I have ever met. It boils down to this; if it wasn't Lizzie, then who else could it have been? The answer is nobody, hence it was Lizzie."

"I was outraged by Fall River ostracising Lizzie after her acquittal and I suppose I was hoping that she was indeed innocent, but I can see the logic of your arguments."

"Thank you. Amongst all the confusing and contradictory statements that have been our life these past two days, there is a piece of testimony which rings true and for me is the most chilling aspect of these murders."

"Which testimony is that or should I say, whose?"

"It came from Bridget. She said, if you recall, that when she went to let Andrew Borden in she distinctly heard Lizzie laugh upstairs. This is a woman who has just slaughtered her stepmother and is awaiting her father's return to dispatch him also, yet she is heard laughing. I cannot bring to my mind any image which fills me with so much horror as Lizzie Borden…laughing."

Although I had read Bridget's testimony, the fact of Lizzie laughing had passed me by, but when I thought of it now, I shuddered. I began to fervently wish that Lizzie would not be in attendance when we had our audience with Emma. I had no wish to look into those unyielding eyes again.

All too soon we found ourselves standing outside 'Maplecroft'. I barely had the time to withdraw my hand from the door after rapping on it before Mrs Courtenay Gray opened it.

"Good morning, gentlemen, Miss Emma is in the library. May I take your coats and hats?" she asked us in such a way as to suggest that entry over the threshold would be permanently denied if we failed to remove the articles in question. After divesting ourselves of said items, Mrs Gray ushered us into the presence of Emma Borden once more. I was relieved to see that Emma was alone.

"Mr Holmes, Dr Watson, good morning, please take a seat."

"How is your sister? Recovered from her ordeal I trust?" asked Holmes.

"She has said little about it and I have not pressed her for I know better than to do so. If she feels the need to unburden herself then she will. We have periods of being close, but more usually than not we live quite separate lives. Speaking of my sister, have you news for me, Mr Holmes?"

"The good doctor and I have pored over the official records in great detail. We found it most informative. It has certainly allowed me to look at the case in a different light and given me some fresh insights. In short, it has been an enlightening experience for me to be here in Fall River and to connect so closely with those sad events of five years ago."

"Apologies, Mr Holmes, but none of that means anything to me. I believe you are fudging the issue. Have you come to a conclusion regarding my sister's guilt or innocence?"

"Have you?"

"I wanted an answer from you, Mr Holmes, not a question."

"I was unable to come to a conclusion. The jury were undoubtedly right, given the evidence presented to them, to acquit you sister."

"It's your opinion I desire not facts, Mr Holmes."

"The facts reflect my opinion, Miss Borden, I find myself quite unable to reach, just like the jury, a verdict as regards Lizzie."

Emma stood up and paced around the room, staring straight ahead, displaying some inner torment on her features. She returned to her seat.

"Gentlemen, you may leave the house. Thank you for your time, but not your obfuscation."

I rose and started to say something, but Holmes shook his head. "Come, Watson. Goodbye Miss Borden."

Emma Borden turned and gazed out of the window. We were well and truly dismissed. As we walked into the hall I heard a sound from the direction of the stairs and saw Lizzie standing there, smiling. I shivered and followed Holmes out into Queen Street.

"She knew that you thought Lizzie guilty, Holmes."

"I expected she would and I am convinced more than ever that she concurs with that view."

"Why, if that is the case, does she remain living there with Lizzie?"

"Perhaps she has no-one else; perhaps she has sympathy with Lizzie."

"But her own father was murdered, Holmes."

"Indeed, it appears unfathomable does it not that Emma would continue living with her sister, but it may well be a union that does not last. Time will tell."

"Why did she ask you to look into the case I wonder?"

"Somewhere inside, she may have a shred of doubt and if I could have boosted that doubt then life may have come easier for her. Emma is a deeply unhappy woman and needs assurances where there are none and can be none."

"I can see that neither of them will ever have peace, the events of the past will be an ever-present. By the way, did you see…?"

"Yes I saw her, another chilling image to sit beside the other."

We saw no need to delay our journey back to New York, Fall River had nothing now to detain us. A visit to the offices of the Fall River Line resulted in tickets for New York on the *Puritan* which was sailing later in the day. We sought out Elmer Hogan to say our farewells, his nephew was nowhere to be found although he would be back in New York himself in a few days, ready to act as Holmes's 'lieutenant'. We settled our account with Peter Jubb and with a backward glance at 92 Second Street; we prepared to take our leave of Fall River.

STEAMER PRISCILLA.

Length over all, 440 feet 6 inches; length on water line, 423 feet 6 inches; breadth over guards, 93 feet; breadth of hull, 52 feet 6 inches; depth of hull, molded, 21 feet 6 inches; draft of water, light, 12 feet 6 inches. Registered gross tonnage, 5,292.

Chapter Seventeen

The *Puritan* was no less splendid and comfortable than her sister ship the *Priscilla* and the voyage, what little I knew of it, was exceedingly calm and uneventful. We had eaten before boarding the vessel and I, for one, was ready to sleep and after a few brief words of no import over a brandy, I retired for the evening. My sleep however was fitful and disturbed and I still felt very much as I had the evening before as we steamed into New York.

Holmes joined me on deck and we gazed at the now familiar New York skyline, drenched in early morning autumn sunshine. The new buildings springing up reminded me of new shoots bursting forth from the soil and forcing their way upwards in the first days of spring.

"A city of grand ideas needs equally grand statements of its worth. These buildings we see now, growing like stalks toward the sky are surely just the beginning; future generations will gaze on sights that we can only imagine."

"It just seems unnatural to my eyes, Holmes."

"Progress, my boy, progress."

"If that's what you wish to call it."

There was a line of cabs on the quayside as we disembarked, their drivers shouting and calling to each other with each one trying to outdo the other with their use of profanities. In their defence, it did all seem very light-hearted and no one was taking offence or as far as I could ascertain, taking any notice whatsoever. Our cabbie was of that breed of New York driver who had scant regard for their own safety and even less for that of their fare-paying passengers. He did display, however, a rare skill in negotiating the morning traffic. In that situation I quickly came to the realisation that not having any form of patience was actually a virtue when it came to delivering one's fares as quickly as possible to their destination, avoiding the many canvas-covered wagons, small carts loaded down with freight and an endless stream of cabs, bicycles and pedestrians.

Our destination was of course the Belle Vue Hotel and we arrived just as the remains of breakfast were being cleared away.

Lavinia Kuhns greeted us as though we had been away travelling the continent for a year or more, throwing her arms around me and attempting with no measure of success, to do the same with Holmes.

"Gentlemen, you should have wired to let me know you were coming. Still, no harm done, you sit yourselves down and I'll rustle something up for you. And you'll never guess who was here just a short while ago; my brother-in-law, well my ex brother-in-law to be exact, Sidney. Did I tell you about him? Well, he was married to my sister, Violet, but between you and me, he always favoured me and was always devising ways to be in my company, not that I encouraged him in any way. Well, I wouldn't would I? Violet was my sister and as I always say, kin is kin no matter who they are. Anyway, marriage to my sister did not suit either one and Violet took up with a banker who took her off to Alabama. Not seen or heard from her for years, but blow me, the last person I expected to see was Sidney, not having been family proper, shall we say, for these past twelve years. He runs a general store in Hoboken now, done very well for himself, gents, but I reckon he still has a soft spot for me. I could tell by the way he looked at me over the coffee pot. What do you think, Frank?"

Frank Kuhns merely sighed and carried on with his task of collecting plates and cutlery as his wife ended her mercifully short tale and followed Frank into the kitchen to prepare something for us.

After we had eaten we discussed our plans for the day and the coming week. Holmes still had a few days left to him before taking up the educational cudgel once more and I was hoping we could visit some of the city's museums and galleries, something I had singularly failed to do thus far. Holmes was positively enthusiastic about the plan and we started to map out our itinerary with the aid of a guide book the Kuhns kept for visitor's use.

We accomplished this mission over the next few days and became quite skilled at tramping the broad avenues of the mesmerising city. Once Holmes had returned to the college and it became apparent that the NYPB was not going to call on my services in my previous guise as police surgeon then my thoughts began to turn towards home. As much as I might have enjoyed spending months traversing America, I felt that London was calling me.

Sherlock Holmes understood my restlessness and bore me no ill-will if I were to choose to return to England. He assured me that Hogan and McMullen being able lieutenants may well have the effect of shortening his own stay.

On the occasion of my last night in New York, Holmes treated me to a sumptuous meal at Louis Sherry's restaurant at 37th Street and 5th Avenue. The eatery was exceedingly popular with what was termed 'The Four Hundred' who represented the elite of New York society and rightly so in my opinion. The following morning therefore I found myself, ticket in hand, waiting to board the ship that would take me across the Atlantic. Holmes and I shook hands and I wished him well for the rest of his tenure in New York and I expressed my hope that when he returned home he would be positively brimming with tales of the Kuhns family to regale me with.

My nights during the voyage were filled with dreams of floating torsos and axe murders. My last night's sleep however was to be disturbed only by a dream of 221b Baker Street.

****

A few notes.....

William Guldensuppe

Guldensuppe was one of roughly one hundred murder victims in New York in 1897, and the dismembering of a lowly immigrant would not necessarily rate much attention in a city with 3.4 million souls. But news eggheads regard 1897 as the most sallow of New York's infamous era of yellow journalism, with Hearst's Evening Journal and Pulitzer's World frothing to pummel one another over unsavoury crime stories. And that is how the case of the humble scattered Dutchman became a sensation. Hearst assigned a platoon of scribes to the case, including George Arnold, the Journal's most dogged newshound. Detectives began tailing him just to keep up. Guldensuppe had lived in Hell's Kitchen; in a small rooming house on Ninth Ave. near 34th St. The Hearst papers leased the entire building to keep the competition away.

Reporter Arnold soon discerned that Guldensuppe had been more than a tenant to the landlady, a native Dane named Augusta Nack who worked as a midwife for German speakers in the neighbourhood. Guldensuppe had moved into the Nack household about 16 months earlier and soon replaced Herman Nack, a bread deliveryman, in the master bedroom. When the husband moved out, a second tenant, barber Martin Thorn, moved in. By asking around the building, Arnold learned that Guldensuppe and Thorn were often at each other's throats - apparently over the affections of their landlady. Guldensuppe had beaten Thorn senseless at least twice, and eyewitness saw Thorn pull a gun on the rubber during a third confrontation. The Journal smelled a love triangle, and Arnold caught Augusta Nack in a series of lies about her relationship with Guldensuppe. At Arnold's urging, detectives escorted the woman to police headquarters. In her corset they found $340, withdrawn from her bank account in the days after Guldensuppe's disappearance. Her travel trunk was freshly packed, and she had begun making inquiries about steamship passage to Europe. The woman said she thought she was being abandoned by Guldensuppe and could not afford to live in New York alone. Meanwhile, authorities arrested Thorn, who was trying to slip across the border into Canada.

Tips soon led the Hearst men to a farm in Woodside, Queens, where the owner said a couple matching the descriptions of Thorn and Nack had rented a cottage there just before Guldensuppe was killed. The farmer noted that wastewater from the cottage had formed a blood-red puddle beneath its bathtub drainpipe. On an editor's hunch, Hearst minions began canvassing dry good stores in Queens. At Riger's in Long Island City, they found oilcloth of the identical flowered design used to wrap Guldensuppe's remains. The owner's wife said a German-speaking woman of Nack's build had purchased the cloth.

The next day, Hearst's paper howled in a banner headline: 'MURDER MYSTERY SOLVED BY THE JOURNAL!' It credited 'the best editorial brains in the world' and gave reporter Arnold the $1,000 reward that Hearst had put up. Thorn denied all, but Nack scotched that strategy by confessing. She said Guldensuppe had caught her in bed with Thorn several times, and the big rubber had thrashed the smaller barber. The couple rented the cottage for the murder, and she lured the Dutchman there with a promise of sex. Instead, Thorn stuck a blade in his heart and cut him up in the bathtub. They wrapped the body and dumped it in the East River. The head, encased in plaster, never surfaced. Thorn remained mute, but the talkative Nack was unapologetic, explaining that Guldensuppe had an active life of "intrigue" with many women while she was expected to be faithful to him. They were both convicted. Thorn was sentenced to the electric chair. He went to his death Aug. 1, 1898, at Sing Sing, clutching a crucifix in an execution the press called "a success in every particular." The confession saved Nack's hide. She was sentenced to fifteen years but served just nine.

Lizzie Borden

The Borden murders and the resulting trial was a sensation at the time and has held a fascination ever since. New books (not to mention TV shows, movies and even songs) on the slayings occur at regular intervals and new theories still crop up from time to time. Officially of course, the case remains unsolved and that is how it will always remain. Chief among the theories are these: Lizzie herself, despite her acquittal. One writer proposed that she committed the murders while in a fugue state, while mystery author Ed McBain, in his 1984 novel *Lizzie*, had Borden committing the murders after being caught in a lesbian tryst with the maid. McBain speculated that Mrs Borden had caught Lizzie and maid Bridget Sullivan together and had reacted with horror and disgust, and that Lizzie had killed Mrs Borden with a candlestick; when her father returned she had confessed to him, but he had reacted to her revelation of the affair exactly as Mrs Borden had and in a rage she had gotten one of the hatchets and killed him with it, with Bridget disposing of the hatchet somewhere afterward. (In her later years, Lizzie Borden was rumoured to be a lesbian, but there was no such speculation about Sullivan, who found other employment after the murders and later married a man.) One prominent theory suggests that Lizzie was physically and sexually abused by her father. Bridget Sullivan allegedly gave a deathbed confession to her sister, stating that she had changed her testimony on the stand in order to protect Lizzie.

A "William Borden", Andrew Borden's illegitimate son, a butcher and horse meat trader who may have tried and failed to extort money from his father. This theory is advanced by Arnold Brown in his book *Lizzie Borden: The Legend, the Truth, the Final Chapter*.

Emma Borden, having established an alibi at Fairhaven, Massachusetts (about 15 miles away from Fall River) comes secretly to Fall River to commit the murders and returns to Fairhaven to receive the telegram informing her of the murders.

John Morse, Lizzie's maternal uncle, rarely met with the family after his sister died, but came to stay with them the night before the murders. He was considered a suspect by police for a period of time.

After the trial, the sisters moved into a large, modern house in the neighbourhood called "The Hill" in Fall River. Around this time, Lizzie began using the name Lizbeth A. Borden. At their new house, which Lizbeth named 'Maplecroft,' the sisters had a staff that included live-in maids, a housekeeper, and a coachman. Because Abby was ruled to have died before Andrew, her estate went first to Andrew and then, at his death, passed to his daughters as part of his estate; a considerable settlement, however, was paid to settle claims by Abby's family (especially Abby's two sisters). In 1897, Lizzie was charged with the theft of two paintings, valued at less than one hundred dollars, from the Tilden-Thurber store in Fall River. The controversy was privately resolved. In 1904, Lizzie met a young actress, Nance O'Neil, and for the next two years, Lizzie and Nance were inseparable. About this time, Emma moved out of Maplecroft, presumably offended by her sister's relationship with the actress, which included at least one lavish catered party for Nance and her theatrical company. Emma stayed with the family of Reverend Buck and sometime around 1915, moved to Newmarket, New Hampshire, living quietly and virtually anonymously in a house she had presumably purchased for two sisters, Mary and Annie Conner.

Lizzie died on June 1, 1927, at the age of 67, after a long illness from complications following gall bladder surgery. Emma died nine days later, as a result of a fall down the back stairs of her house in Newmarket. They were buried together in the family plot, along with a sister who had died in early childhood, their mother, their stepmother, and their headless father. Both Lizzie and Emma left their estates to charitable causes; Lizzie's being left predominately to animal care organizations, Emma's to various humanitarian organizations in Fall River. Bridget Sullivan died in 1948, more than twenty years after the death of the Borden sisters, in Butte, Montana.

Fact/Fiction

There is a blurring in this book of fact and fiction, both in the text and the photographs. To clarify:

Ameer Ben Ali was convicted of the second-degree murder of Carrie Brown and after serving eleven years in prison was released and he left the USA for Algeria.

The *SS Bremen*'s maiden voyage was as detailed. She was re-named *King Alexander* in 1922 and scrapped in 1929.

The fire that Holmes and Watson observe on Ellis Island was very destructive. The immigration offices there were not to re-open for three years.

Wilson Hargreave was a creation of Arthur Conan Doyle as was the NYPB which, more properly should be styled the NYPD. There was a serving police officer named James O' Connell, but from a later time.

Frank and Lavinia Kuhns (and her extended family!) and the Belle Vue Hotel are entirely fictitious as is the police training college and therefore Eugene Seitz.

The Fall River Line operated between 1847 and 1937. The *Puritan* first saw service in 1889 and the *Priscilla* in 1894.

Chief Elmer Hogan and his nephew, Michael Hogan are fictional. All other Fall River police officers of Fall River including Marshal Rufus B Hilliard were indeed serving officers.

Sansom Weinberger, Charlie Walters and Honoria Walters are fictitious as is Peter Jubb although Walter Jubb was real enough and had connections with Lizzie as detailed.

Carr's Perfumery did not exist and I am not aware of a perfume called 'Midnight in Paris', but you would think there must have been!

The Metacomet Mill was built by Richard Borden in 1847 and was one of Fall River's largest employers.

The Borden house at 92 Second Street is now a Bed and Breakfast establishment and very popular, especially with ghost hunters who are attracted to the house by tales of paranormal happenings there.

'Maplecroft' on French Street, Lizzie's home for the rest of her life is a private residence now, although the current owner did try running and a Bed and Breakfast business there too.

Views

I have invited other authors to air their views on the Borden murders. But before we come to those, here is mine:

I first read of the Borden case when I was eleven or twelve, I cannot recall which book it was, however. Whilst not having a special interest in the case, I did pick up the occasional book on the subject, all of which had something to offer by way of fresh insights or new suspects. None of them has ever swayed me from my initial view that Lizzie Borden must have been the culprit. The cumulative effect of the 'evidence' against her is overpowering. Simply put, it had to be her. My views have been expressed through Holmes and like Holmes, I find the account by Bridget Sullivan of hearing Lizzie laughing upstairs to be very, very chilling.

This the view of Tom Turley, author of Sherlock Holmes and the Tainted Canister:

I'm not sure I could give you a definite answer, even if tied down, but in my opinion either Lizzie committed the murders or she knew who did. Leaving aside Bridget Sullivan's so-called "deathbed confession," the only alternative--as Lizzie claimed when notifying a neighbour of her father's death--was that "somebody [Emma Borden? William Borden? John Morse? Jack the Ripper?] came in and killed him." If so, the murderer would have had to stay inside the house-- unseen by either Lizzie or the maid--for over an hour after killing Abby Borden. Lizzie's testimony at the inquest (excluded at her trial) was so confused and contradictory that even a friendly coroner had to conclude that she was "probably guilty." Her bizarre behaviour before, during, and after the murders--which she never satisfactorily explained--was not dissimilar to other strange incidents before and after 1892. Victoria Lincoln, who knew a lot about the family and wrote sympathetically of Lizzie, had no doubt at all about her guilt. I agree with with Ms. Lincoln's basic thesis: that Lizzie was always a bit "off," whether from epilepsy (as she posits) or from some other illness. Lizzie's mother, who died young, was subject (according to Ms. Lincoln) to "severe migraines and seizures of apparently unmotivated rage."

    Lizzie would have had plenty of motivation for her own rage. From all accounts I've read, the atmosphere at 92 Second Street was downright poisonous by August, 1892. Andrew Borden was a rich old skinflint who refused his family indoor plumbing and forced them to eat week-old soup. Just before his death, he promised to share part of his daughters' inheritance with Abby Borden's sisters, with the result that neither Lizzie nor Emma was speaking to their stepmother. Andrew had butchered Lizzie's pigeons when she was a girl; yet, he paid for her voyage to England two years before the murders. This ambiguous, love/hate relationship--and Lizzie's "lack of affect" stemming from her mother's early death--made her a prime candidate for parricide, according to the psychological articles I've read. On a different level, The Legend of Lizzie Borden (an excellent 1975 television drama, starring Elizabeth Montgomery and Fritz Weaver) hinted at every possibility from necrophilia to incest, with Lizzie committing the murders in the nude(!).

The views of Stephen Seitz, author of Sherlock Holmes and the Plague of Dracula, Never Meant To Be (a Holmes novel) and the Ace Herron mysteries:

    Andrew Borden may have sexually abused both his daughters; the house is designed to give him access to his daughters' bedrooms without his second wife knowing. He was also a cheap bastard who didn't even have running water in the house, and he seldom gave the girls, who had aged beyond the likelihood of marriage, any money. Lizzie also hated her stepmother so much, she couldn't even address her by name. Lizzie always called her 'Mrs. Borden.' Motive: plenty.
    After the murders, the hatchet was found with the handle broken off and the blade cleaned. Lizzie was also seen burning a

dress. The day before the attacks, she tried to buy some prussic acid at the local drugstore. Anyone interested in aiding the police would not be destroying evidence. Finally, nobody else could have done it. Bridget, the maid, was working upstairs at the time and had no reason to kill her employers. Those in favour of the random stranger theory have no evidence to back it up. By the process of elimination, only Lizzie Borden could have killed her parents.

Here is Luke Kuhns's take. Luke is the author of Sherlock Holmes: Studies in Legacy and The Untold Adventures of Sherlock Holmes.

Lizzie very well could have killed her father and stepmother. Her relationship with her father and stepmother was unstable. Both her and her sister were emotionally neglected, plus his tight grip on the family wealth could point to Lizzie wanting a bit of the family money. Her father was certainly very stingy.

While it wasn't used in the trial the purchasing of the prussic acid is suspicious. What did she intend to do with that? Odd. I have a problem with her mental stability though. Her quickly changing statements as to where she was when the murders happened is also odd. Did she snap, see red, and commit the murders? Or was she just scared and couldn't keep her stories straight. We can't really tell though. The lack of forensic evidence is to thank for that. The local authorities didn't seem to put all the efforts into the case and left Lizzie, if she was the killer, too much time to cover tracks. Burning a dress with 'paint'?

In my opinion Lizzie was likely the axe wielding murder, pushed by a mixture of poor treatment from her father and stepmother, capital gain, and mental instability. I do wonder if she acted alone or was someone whispering things to her? Will we ever know the truth?

Elizabeth Engstrom is the author of *Lizzie Borden*, one of the best of all the books about the Borden murders. Visit *www.elizabethengstrom.com* for details of all her work. You will not be disappointed:

Obviously, there is much mystery surrounding the entire Borden family, not just the murders. Shenanigans took place in that small, stinky house all the time, and secrecy ruled. Everything that is known about the family can be gleaned only from sensationalist newspaper reports after the murders, and trial transcripts, where Lizzie was found not guilty of murdering her father and stepmother.

But reading between the lines, there is a wealth of information in these sources. Surely, we have to take a few leaps from the facts to the theories of what happened on that happy family day, and new theories appear every year. In my book, Lizzie Borden, I take a less-than-conventional leap, but while my resulting theory may be open to discussion, the facts of the case, as related in the book are sound.

Stepmother, Abby Borden had to die first, because then Andrew Borden inherited her estate, and then when he died, Lizzie and Emma inherited his estate. Had Andrew died first, then Abby would have inherited, and her subsequent murder would not have benefitted Lizzie and Emma at all. So starting with that simple fact, the event seems to be far more premeditated than many contemporary theories would postulate. Of course there is always the possibility that the maid or someone outside of the household did the deed, but then there is the question of motive. A continuing, ongoing, fascinating, mystery.

Steven Ehrman offers his view. Steven is the author of the excellent 'Sherlock Holmes Uncovered Tales'. www.amazon.com/Steven-Ehrman :

Lizzie Borden. What images does the name conjure up? Does a children's chant come to mind? The lurid axe murder of Lizzie Borden's father and step-mother has fascinated mystery lovers spanning three centuries. Lizzie was suspected from nearly the start of the investigation into the murders and was indeed charged, yet she was found not guilty. Notwithstanding this verdict the murders cast a pall over not just Lizzie, but a host of secondary suspects such as, her sister, a maid and a visiting uncle. The father was reputed to be a hard and grasping man and had a host of potential assassins.

What would have happened if Sherlock Holmes had been involved in the case? Would the great detective been able to pierce the mystery that befell Fall River?

Acknowledgements etc

There is a wealth of information available on the Borden murders, less so on the Guldensuppe case. One of the most informative and comprehensive websites is http://lizziebordenwarpsandwefts.com/ which is dotted with articles, photographs of Lizzie and her life. It also successfully conjures up how Fall River society conducted itself at that time. A one-stop website definitely. Should you wish to experience the house for yourself then *https://lizzie-borden.com/* is the place for you; bed and breakfast at the Borden house.

Thanks to Stephen Seitz, Luke Kuhns, Tom Turley, Elizabeth Engstrom and Steve Ehrman for sharing their views and allowing me to air them. The consensus among them is that Lizzie Borden was guilty as charged. It's difficult to gainsay it. But what are we left with; at the end of the day we still have an officially unsolved murder although we also have Lizzie…*laughing*.

Thanks as ever to Gill, who spent a Sunday afternoon ploughing through the majority of this book and making corrections and additions as necessary. I am always happy to hand over this particular baton to Gill for I know the changes will be for the better!

Thanks to Steve at MX Publishing and Bob Gibson of Staunch for another great cover.

Later in the year, look out for *Sherlock Holmes and the Scarborough Affair*, a collaboration with Gill Stammers. It is a tale of strong women, chambermaids, sisters, spying, murder and cricket!

David Ruffle Lyme Regis 2015

Links

www.seitzbooks.com

www.lukebenjamenkuhns.wordpress.com

www.elizabethengstrom.com

www.amazon.com/StevenEhrman

www.mxpublishing.co.uk

www.storiesfromlymelight.blogspot.com

www.lizziebordenwarpsandwefts.com

Also from David Ruffle

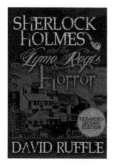  

Sherlock Holmes and The Lyme Regis Trilogy

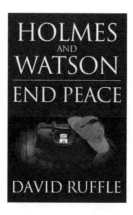

Holmes and Watson – End Peace

www.mxpublishing.com

Also from MX Publishing

MX Publishing is the world's largest specialist Sherlock Holmes publisher, with over a hundred titles and fifty authors creating the latest in Sherlock Holmes fiction and non-fiction.

From traditional short stories and novels to travel guides and quiz books, MX Publishing cater for all Holmes fans.

The collection includes leading titles such as *Benedict Cumberbatch In Transition* and *The Norwood Author* which won the 2011 Howlett Award (Sherlock Holmes Book of the Year).

MX Publishing also has one of the largest communities of Holmes fans on Facebook with regular contributions from dozens of authors.

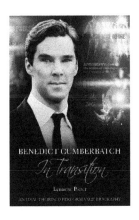

www.mxpublishing.com

Also from MX Publishing

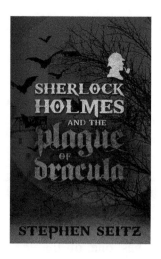

After Mina Murray asks Sherlock Holmes to locate her fiancee, Holmes and Watson travel to a land far eerier than the moors they had known when pursuing the Hound of the Baskervilles. The confrontation with Count Dracula threatens Holmes' health, his sanity, and his life. Will Holmes survive his battle with Count Dracula?

www.mxpublishing.com

Also from MX Publishing

Internationally bestselling traditional short story collections from Luke Kuhns

The Untold Adventures of Sherlock Holmes

Sherlock Holmes Studies In Legacy

www.mxpublishing.com

Also from MX Publishing

"Phil Growick's, 'The Secret Journal of Dr Watson', is an adventure which takes place in the latter part of Holmes and Watson's lives. They are entrusted by HM Government (although not officially) and the King no less to undertake a rescue mission to save the Romanovs, Russia's Royal family from a grisly end at the hand of the Bolsheviks. There is a wealth of detail in the story but not so much as would detract us from the enjoyment of the story. Espionage, counter-espionage, the ace of spies himself, double-agents, double-crossers...all these flit across the pages in a realistic and exciting way. All the characters are extremely well-drawn and Mr Growick, most importantly, does not falter with a very good ear for Holmesian dialogue indeed. Highly recommended. A five-star effort."
The Baker Street Society

www.mxpublishing.com

Also from MX Publishing

Dozens of short story ebooks

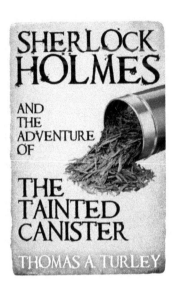

A lost chapter in the Holmes canon finally appears, as Dr. Watson recounts the mystery behind the tragic death of his beloved Mary Morstan. Join him as he attempts to bring a murderer to justice. Along the way, readers will encounter old friends and enemies from several of the other stories, leading to a startling conclusion that may baffle even Sherlock Holmes.

Available via Amazon Kindle, Kobo, Nook and iTunes.

Lightning Source UK Ltd.
Milton Keynes UK
UKHW021348290920
370733UK00010B/2386